"A searing
behind ~~the scenes~~

Set in 1989, this engrossing thriller finds a struggling Hollywood director entangled in a sinister conspiracy. Struggling with a dwindling career and a deteriorating relationship, he lands a job directing a low-budget horror film in Yugoslavia, a nation on the verge of collapse. He finds himself at a crossroads where he must upend all that he's worked for or risk losing the ones he loves.

Kwitny excels at creating atmospheric setting and skillfully manages the intrigue and page-turning plot, sprinkling in plenty of goings-on about the shooting and production work of the movie business along the way.

The plot takes numerous unexpected turns as it builds to a shocking climax.
— *The Prairies Book Review*

Falling Stars over Belgrade **is a searing insider's peek behind the scenes in Hollywood** that takes readers on a roller coaster ride as it depicts what it's like to be a an up-and-coming director hanging on for dear life while trying to build a career.

In the great tradition of Eleanor Coppola's *Notes: On the Making of Apocalypse Now* and Michael Tolkin's *The Player,* **Kwitny's story about a Hollywood director working in a foreign country rings true,** full of the absurdities and misadventures, and manic heartbreak and hope that artists in any field will be able to relate to.
— Eric Jordan Baker, Deluxe Entertainment

Also by Jeffrey Kwitny:

Desolation Lake

A note about the front cover:
Sculptures such as the one shown on the cover of this book
featuring some combination of horses and human figures
are a common sight in many European cities. But the image
of a sculpture depicting a man and a horse grappling in
front of the Parliament building, Belgrade, Serbia, is unique.
Public consensus in Serbia about its meaning seems to be
that the male figure represents common men, naked in front
of power and being ridden and crushed by overbearing
authority. Others contend tend that his position, facing the
horse rather than turning away, is a symbol of resistance.
— *Atlas Obscura*

Falling Stars
over
Belgrade

a novel

Jeffrey Kwitny

LINE BY LINE
BOOKS
LA · CA

Design by Meadowlark Publishing Services.
Cover image of Belgrade Parliament building courtesy of AP—photo by Darko Vojinovic.

Director's chair: ©texelart—Can Stock Photo Inc.

P. vi photo: ©samott—Can Stock Photo Inc..
Author photo: Marcy Kwitny.

Published by Line by Line Books
www.jeffreykwitny.com

Manufactured in the United States of America.

ISBN 978-1-7364166-0-0

Published 2021

For my mother and father—two bright stars
in the firmament

Belgrade Fortress on the confluence of the River Sava and the Danube in an urban area of modern Belgrade, the capital of Serbia.

Тамо где нема жене, нема дома.
Where there is no wife, there is no home.
—Yugoslavian proverb

Is it possible to succeed without any act of betrayal?
—Jean Renoir

ἦθος ἀνθρώπῳ δαίμων
Ethos anthropos daimon
Character is destiny.
—Heraclitus

Prologue

T he flight departed from Los Angeles on a Sunday in February of 1989, the year when revolutions were taking place in far-off lands. The Berlin Wall came down that year. Communism fell in Bulgaria, Czechoslovakia, Romania. Solidarity won elections in Poland. Student-led demonstrations erupted in violence in Tiananmen Square. It was also the year Stephen Krawczyk was hired to direct his first movie. They would shoot the thing in Yugoslavia.

A producer at New Vistas Pictures in West L.A., impressed with Stephen's work, had sent his director's reel to the offices of Starlight Starbright Entertainment S.R.L., located in Rome's exclusive Parioli district outside the Aurelian walls. Max Trueblood, chairman and CEO of Starlight, made horror movies—lots of them. There was a rush to make these films, which were experiencing something of a renaissance at that time. Offerings such as *Nightmare on Elm Street*—budget: $1.8 million, gross: $25 million—spawned legions of spinoffs. In the previous year alone, more than seventy-five horror films had been produced. Trueblood, always on the lookout for American talent, liked *Sucker*, Stephen's 22-minute parody of the Bela

Lugosi version of *Dracula*. The film short, which Stephen had written, directed, photographed and edited, and which he'd shot with an old Bolex 16-millimeter camera, demonstrated real talent—the Roman producer soon offered him a job. But it wasn't only talent that he was scouting for. Investors required American names on the contract—a director's and a star's—if Starlight hoped to get financing and U.S. distribution. The wily businessman knew that even if Stephen failed—this *nessuno di conseguenza*, this American nobody—he could easily replace him. In fact, unbeknownst to Stephen, Trueblood had a nasty reputation in the industry for firing first-time directors and taking control early on.

In Belgrade, where principal photography would take place, Stephen would make a great movie—he was sure of it. He had a priest's pious faith in his own talent. He'd nurtured a dream of becoming a great movie director since boyhood, and he was determined to fulfill it. He *would* succeed. Besides, wasn't that what his mother had always told him? "You can achieve anything you set your mind to, Stephen," she'd said, when he was very little. "Anything imaginable." After he completed the movie, more projects would certainly come his way. And just possibly, he might someday receive a star on the Walk of Fame at the intersection of Hollywood and Vine.

A pipe dream? Many people, thousands, shared this aspiration. Should he have asked for time to reflect before accepting their offer? It was a job directing a real motion picture, the

Holy Grail in Hollywood. Who would have thought for more than a second?

Not in this town.

– PART ONE –
PRE-PRODUCTION

– 1 –

As the airport shuttle van propelled him along the Santa Monica Freeway southbound toward LAX, Stephen looked out the window. The view looked like a zoetrope with images strobing at 24 frames per second. Colossal billboards advertising the new *Batman* movie or the Marlboro Man, tall buildings displaying company logos, Herbalife, the Howard Hughes Center: they flickered past his line of sight. Soon he would ask the driver to take the Venice Boulevard turnoff, a brief detour. Since Stephen was his only passenger that morning, the driver would accommodate him, although Stephen would have to pay extra.

He decided he would end the affair this very morning, before catching his flight to Eastern Europe. He believed that in betraying Elaine he'd torn the fabric that bound the firmament together. He wanted her forgiveness. He wanted their marriage to endure.

Making this movie offered a way to realize a dream, to redeem himself, to mend the cosmic rip, to begin life anew.

•　•　•

His plan was to remain standing near the door of Diane's apartment, ready to make his escape, as he gently broke the news to her. He would be friendly yet somewhat distant as they discussed the separation. There would be tears, no doubt. She would be defiant. She would demand to know what had changed in their relationship. *Did I do something wrong?* she would invariably ask. In any case, that was how it had played on the movie screen in his head for the past week.

He was surprised by what actually happened.

As he walked toward her apartment on that Sunday morning, the Van Go! shuttle driver waiting at the curb, Diane was expecting him; he'd stopped at a pay phone outside a 7-Eleven on the way over and called her. She was used to surprise liaisons like this. When she opened the door, she stood before him, in pajamas of virginal white cotton. She looked bereaved. She sensed what was coming.

It was no wonder: she was a Wiccan goddess with special intuitive powers. Diane belonged to the Pagans & Witches Community, a local coven with over three thousand members that practiced magic in the form of meditation and visualization in addition to occasional spell work. She advocated "free love"; Wicca is a fertility religion.

She offered him coffee. He declined. Their conversation drifted on for a while, mostly small talk: the marine layer along the Southern California coast, they agreed, was unusually gloomy. The couch she'd recently purchased at Pottery Barn was just what her apartment needed. He felt relieved when she finally let him break it off. There were no tears, as it turned out. However, despite appearances, her Goddess powers abandoned her. She collapsed from within, silently.

When it was time to say goodbye, she looked so woeful that he felt compelled to kiss her, which he did, on the lips, hard and fast, more out of a sense of compassion than desire. Unfortunately, as their lips met, he knew instantly that once again he was cheating on his wife.

It was the last time he would kiss Diane Barnes. And just as he was about to make his exit, he noticed the change in her eyes. Her sorrow was replaced by something else: a witch's simmering wrath.

– 2 –

A window seat awaited him in economy class of JAT Airways 107, LAX to JFK to Belgrade Airport. He found it and settled in. He would use the time on the plane to continue annotating the script, which had arrived at their apartment via UPS, encased in a mailing envelope adorned with brightly colored Italian stamps.

"That way you hit the ground running," a man named Colon, sporting a cultured British accent, had explained over the phone. He was Starlight's line producer—the man who would be the production's commander in the trenches. When Stephen heard his voice, he immediately thought of Rex Harrison in *My Fair Lady*. Many of his mental associations were with old movies.

But then the producer's voice dropped into a stage whisper, as if someone might be listening into their conversation: "Actually, just between you and me, the script is rubbish. A bit daft, really. Never mind. It's the dialogue that concerns us. Just rework it a bit, will you, Stephen? Make it sound … well, make it sound *American.*"

Stephen hated the script. It was an incoherent, illogical concoction no doubt dictated by Trueblood to a bilingual assistant whose mastery of English was clearly weedy. Its working title was *Il Vampiro,* but the English-speaking members of the crew referred to it simply as "The Vampire Movie." The plot was predictable. A libidinous vampire, disguised as an elite boarding school headmaster, feeds on the blood of the academy's prettiest coeds—the usual damsel-in-distress horror formula that infected the movie industry during the eighties. Stephen knew what he was signing on for. But that didn't matter. He would have shot a water-heater repair manual, the Los Angeles phone book— anything. Give him enough money, a decent production crew, a functioning 35mm Mitchell movie camera, plenty of Kodak film stock, and a handful of actors and he'd shoot a masterpiece of cinematic genius. Even movies like *Lawrence of Arabia,* he'd reminded himself, bore little resemblance to their original scripts. Francis Ford Coppola was famous for still writing the script while shooting *The Godfather.* Stephen had already rewritten much of *Il Vampiro,* and had faxed drafts with his notes to the executive producer in Rome for comments. Once ensconced in his hotel in Belgrade, he'd continue to make script changes.

That was the plan.

– 3 –

He deplaned at the Belgrade airport. At the bottom of the ramp he was met by two men dressed in gray uniforms. Their uniforms, and especially the slanted military-style hats, reminded Stephen of what SMERSH wore in the James Bond movies.

"Passport control," said one of the men as they flanked him, taking him delicately by the elbows as if Stephen were a fragile, elderly person. "Come with us, sir." Their faces were stony and expressionless, their voices flat. They must be NKVD, the People's Commisariat of Internal Affairs, an agency of the Soviet Union, Stephen assumed—a romantic notion, although they were more likely just regular Yugoslav airport police. Characters, he decided, straight out of Central Casting.

Stephen had no time to consider his options. Because the men looked stern and robotic, he resisted the urge to ask questions.

They led him unhurriedly around the crush of passengers forming lines at the passport checkpoint and ushered him into a small, nearly empty room. There were no pictures on the gray walls. Only a small Ikea pressed-board desk and two cheap plastic chairs, one behind and one in front. One of the two officers—they appeared nearly identical in their uniforms—gestured toward a chair. Stephen sat.

"Your passport," demanded the man next to the chair. The man's English was very good: carefully enunciated words, each syllable deliberate, mirroring the soldierly body language. He extended his hand toward Stephen, who unzipped a small side pocket of his bag where he carried his initialed boarding ticket and his passport. The man took the passport and left the room while his partner remained behind, standing inert near the door, staring into space, indifferent.

Stephen worried. He felt the first symptoms of a migraine coming on—flashes of light, tingling on the left side of his face. He did not want to succumb to despair. He must remain calm. He must ignore the increasing pain and be strong.

Neither Stephen nor the policeman at the door spoke during the half hour they waited. Then:

"Thank you, sir," said the other policeman as he reentered the tiny room, bearing the passport that was Stephen's greatest protection, his Achilles' shield in this Eastern European country. Leaning over, almost bowing slightly, he handed it respectfully to Stephen. Once again, he took the American director by the elbow, pointing to the door. "This way, sir."

Beyond the bulletproof glass partition that separated

the passport clearance area from a throng of waiting friends and relatives was a thin man, gaunt like a soldier just back from a war, wearing a gray, tweedy sport jacket one size too large. With his lean build, a face reddened by thousands of broken capillaries and ginger hair, he reminded Stephen of a rusty nail. The man was waving a small cardboard sign in his hands. In block letters, hand-drawn in black marker pen ink, was the word STEPHEN. Stephen caught his eye and waved.

"You must be the driver!" he called out, advancing toward the stranger. He realized his voice sounded unnaturally loud and high-pitched, like an excited child. He made a mental note to monitor the tone and volume of his voice at all times. Stay calm, he reminded himself. Be in control. Be *directorial*.

The man grinned, his mouth oddly crooked, revealing sharp yellow teeth, and said in a crisp Londoner accent, "No. You are mistaken, I'm afraid. I am your *savior*."

Stephen nodded, blinking. The stranger seemed to relish Stephen's momentary confusion. Although repulsed, Stephen could not refrain from staring at the decaying teeth.

"You … are … Stephen," the Englishman noted, sounding like he was offering Stephen a sweet, perhaps to help the young foreigner recover his wits.

Stephen continued to stare imprudently. The man seemed much younger from a distance, but on closer inspection his brown-spotted, sun-scorched, tree-bark skin added years to his appearance. His voice was no help either. It was raspy, decimated by alcohol, smoking, or both. It was hard to guess his age. He was either a beleaguered seventy or a hideously ravaged forty.

Before Stephen could respond affirmatively, the producer declared:

"I am *Colon,*" he said, as if this were a marvelous revelation, too good to be true. *Voilà!* he seemed to say. As if the name meant *everything,* as if he were introducing a star at the Oscars. *Ladies and gentlemen, the winner of the 1989 Academy Award for Best Actor—Colon!* "C-O-L-O-N," he continued, spelling it out in a long-suffering tone. The grin had vanished as quickly as a swatted fly. "As in Cologne, Germany. *Not* the large intestine." Still frowning, he extended a bony hand and Stephen shook it. "Furthermore, in response to your supposition regarding my role, I am nobody's *driver,*" he snarled. "I have a car, or at least some banger the locals *call* a car. But you will address me always as your *producer.*"

Stephen nodded gravely. He wondered: would he call him Mister Producer? He wasn't even sure if Colon was his first or last name. That was how they'd referred to him at the production office. They gave him little information about this man, and Stephen decided it would be sensible not to ask.

He had dealt with producers of Colon's ilk before. There are producers out there, he'd discovered, who view themselves as the *real* directors, the *true* artists, the ones who put the disparate elements of the production together, who managed the unwieldy assemblage, who wrote the checks and divvied out cash, made all the big day-to-day production decisions. To them, directors were bit players, hired hands who merely did their bidding. (Stephen had heard the infamous Alfred Hitchcock quote; everyone in Hollywood seemed to know it. One evening at Norma Shearer's home the great director pulled himself up portentously and announced to the roomful of guests, "All actors are cattle." Some producers would say the same about directors.) Stephen knew that producers could be modest and accommodating, decent enough people, but for others, this was deceptive, a ploy: they *seemed* friendly, but they were projecting the phony affability of a mortuary salesman. *We have this white mother-of-pearl cremation urn, on sale now for only $875.*

"Nice to meet you," said Stephen warily.

"They put you through the wringer back there?"

"At customs? Kind of. It was nothing."

"Yes, of course they did. You are a Big American Film Director. They were expecting you. *Is Beôgrad,* not Burbank." He pronounced the city's name in what Stephen assumed must be his best Serbian accent: heavy, guttural, almost a growl. "The White City," the producer added with a smirk. "Pure as the saints above."

But to Stephen it was a very exotic, romantic-sounding word: *Beôgrad.*

"You are visiting royalty here, and you should behave like it. Tell people what to do, Stephen. Order them about. Bully them a little. Act like you are *The Man* Tito himself. And no need to worry at all. They checked your passport and ran a security check. INTERPOL and all that. You are good to go." Then after a deliberate beat for dramatic effect, looking about furtively, bringing his mouth close to Stephen's ear, whispering conspiratorially as if Orwell's Thought Police were listening in, he added, "Otherwise, you'd be in jail right now ..."

Stephen chuckled nervously.

"... and off to the labor camps you'd go, you'd go!" he sang brightly, as if he were reciting a nursery rhyme. The small yellow teeth were once again on display. The hobgoblin smile had returned.

Stephen smiled weakly. The producer went on drolly:

"Yugoslavia has had its own bloody labor camps" — stated with a wink and a nod. "Even though it's *supposedly* broken its ties with Moscow." But then, his good mood abruptly changing, he looked at Stephen sternly. "But *you* know all this, of course. You've done your homework."

Stephen strained to maintain a poker face: he hadn't. A feeling of trepidation was beginning to radiate from his center. But he needed to appear strong and confident — directorial.

"I've done a little—"

"But that was then," interrupted Colon, taking Stephen's arm and guiding him toward the exit. *Everyone seems to want to guide me along like I'm enfeebled.* "For now, let's get you to baggage claim ... before they change their minds."

– 4 –

As Colon drove to the hotel, Stephen gazed out the window at the gray, monolithic, concrete buildings that panned across his field of vision like a tracking shot in a movie.

He commented as supportively as he could on the view—"Charmingly gritty"—figuring he'd better project a positive attitude from then on. Stephen understood that Colon was effectively the eyes and ears of the executive producer, the man who would report back to Rome every move Stephen made—every word spoken, his attitude, everything—as if Stephen were Spartacus and his boss Crassus.

"Yes … *charming* indeed," replied Colon, voice laced with sarcasm.

"Well, what I mean is, some of the architecture is pretty interesting," Stephen said weakly, an attempt at diplomacy. "I've never seen anything like it."

"It's all Art Nouveau. Bauhaus. Neo-Byzantine," Colon responded, as his tiny Yugo sputtered along the Bulevar

Arsenija Čarnojevića on the 18-kilometer drive into the old city. Colon glanced at his neophyte director in the seat next to him. Stephen was silent, turned inward, gazing wanly out the window, struggling to curb feelings of dread. "Until you get to the *blokovi,* that is," Colon continued. "The apartment blocks of *Novi Beôgrad.*"

Stephen turned to him. "Novi?"

"New. Or used to be, anyway. By *their* standards. A real cock-up of a place if you ask me."

Cock-up of a place. Stephen eyed the man suspiciously. Colon's accent was pure BBC, cultured British. Slang phrases like this one, however, were direct from Liverpool.

"Ah! The Danube. I always think of Strauss's waltz," responded Stephen, perking up. "Now that I've said it, I won't be able to get the tune out of my head. Or the image from *2001* either. The bone turning into a spaceship?"

"There are *two* rivers, Stephen, as I'm sure you know," Colon stated with a withering glare. *"That,* sir, is the Sava, not your ..." He cleared his throat. "... blue Danube"—pursing his lips mockingly.

"Got it," said Stephen, his small smile vanishing.

"And it's not blue. It's muddy gray. Anyway, it went all to pot. Now the city's this bloody monstrosity. Even the local blokes don't like it much."

"Like something out of *Blade Runner,*" Stephen offered. It was a film he greatly admired.

"Yes indeedy. Very good." Stephen had been temporarily forgiven. "Rick Deckard would feel right at home here," Colon added, asserting his film history expertise.

"What about the *old* city?"

"Heavily bombed by the Luftwaffe in Forty-one," Colon answered, smiling. Hard to tell if he were more in awe of the fact or of his own expertise. "Think of it. Twenty-four thousand souls erased from the earth. Just like that. Poof! Gone!"

He snapped his fingers. Stephen's blood went hot.

"My guess?" continued the producer. "Built quick and cheap. That's how they did things. The monstrous legacy of Communist rule."

Like this movie, thought Stephen. *Quick and cheap. The monstrous legacy of Italian filmmaking.*

As they drove on, Colon remaining silent for the remainder of the journey, Stephen became circumspect. He had much to worry about. He'd received over the phone a briefing from the production office in Rome about the difficulties he'd encounter here, besides the obvious language and cultural differences. There was the minuscule budget, but that was expected—it was a B-movie. They'd hired mostly amateur actors who worked cheap—the crew, even cheaper. He learned that some of the actors were young, bilingual American expatriates with no acting experience whatsoever, holed up in Rome, working regular jobs—cashiers, secretaries, delivery drivers, sometimes models—but registered with the local talent agency. They were well aware of the need for American actors: a priceless commodity in the Italian film industry. They knew they could make more money in a week of acting than in a month of assembling Big Macs at the McDonald's in the Piazza di Spagna. One of the actors, a 25-year-old named Ron Stiltz, had fared better than the others, opening the equivalent of a Trader Joe's with money borrowed from his parents. It was a business model unheard of in Rome at the time—frozen, packaged, ready-made meals for working-class people on the run. The locals, especially the younger generation, working longer hours than ever, welcomed a convenience store that offered cheap, relatively healthy products—goods with a long shelf life—and fled the leafy stalls at the Campo de' Fiori in droves. The young entrepreneur signed with the agency not because he needed the money—he was relatively well off—but because he enjoyed acting in horror films.

Meanwhile, the "star" of the movie, Kurt Buckfellow, was hired based on his strong appeal in the foreign markets. His name would sell well overseas, where the big money for action movies was to be had. He'd done *Hell Zone Renegades,* an action flick that made millions for its investors and was South Korea's biggest hit that year. But the fact that Buckfellow bore a distinctly American-sounding name—a fabricated moniker; his real name was Laurence Feigenbaum—helped the producers' cause mightily. His talent at speaking his lines was inconsequential: there was little need for dubbing in action movies, as there was scant dialogue. *Hell Zone* was nearly "pure cinema," as cineastes called picture-storytelling without speech. Violent imagery was the universal language of current action movies.

The rest of the cast and crew consisted of nearly 120 men and women: American expatriates, Yugoslavian and Italian grips and gaffers who spoke little of each other's language, carpenters, artisans, day parts, cooks, secretaries, and extras. Hence, two full-time translators were hired. They would strive valiantly to convey the director's wishes and keep the lines of communication humming.

And then there was the absurdly short 30-day shooting schedule. "Hit-and-run filmmaking," Stephen called it. Film processing, special effects, the inevitable reshoots, inserts, and all other post-production tasks would take place in Rome for weeks after shooting halted in Belgrade. But the biggest challenge was thoroughly apparent to everyone: the director himself had never directed a feature-length movie. From a purely objective standpoint, there was no reason to believe this one would succeed.

The people at Starbright, however, were certain of its financial success. They were not worried at all. They were pragmatic businessmen rather than dreamers like Stephen. There was big money in horror movies, and they knew perfectly well how to make them. They'd made many movies just like *Il Vampiro.* All made money. They followed a formula, a noxious tincture composed of blood, nudity, and supernatural storytelling. They dealt in emotions, not logic. They understood well that their films addressed people's deepest fears on a visceral level rather than a rational one.

Back in the Eternal City—home to Michelangelo's Sistine Chapel ceiling, no less— Trueblood called the shots like a modern-day Pope Julius II. (Max Trueblood was the name he employed in the credits of his movies; his real name was Federico Annunziato.) He was a pudgy runt of a man with a pug face that reminded Stephen of Edward

G. Robinson. A psychologist might suggest he suffered from a Napoleon complex, but he was revered in Italy as a *grande uomo d'affari*—a colossus of a businessman. He'd made his fortune by shooting his first spaghetti horror movie—*Horrifica!*—for $150,000 and turning a profit of $22 million. He was considered by Hollywood insiders, somewhat sardonically (truth be told, they respected anyone who could make money), as "The Italian Roger Corman," a reference to the B-movie maestro of the 60s who was himself known in the industry as the "The Pope of Pop Cinema."

"This movie," the big man announced with great bravado at one production meeting, "will be *un capolavoro!*" A masterpiece. "It will be beeeg-a! You will see. And it had bet-ter show every single li-ra on the beeeg-a silver screen."

Trueblood expected his movie to have the scale of the Charlton Heston epic *Ben-Hur* (filmed largely at Cinecittà Studios in Rome, the largest film studio in Europe), a movie he viewed as a model of great filmmaking. Another of his favorites, *Raiders of the Lost Ark,* was usually mentioned at these meetings as well. (He fashioned himself the Steven Spielberg of Italy.) To accomplish this feat on a $900,000 budget (by comparison, Spielberg made *Raiders* for twenty million, considered a moderately high budget in the eighties), the Italian producers would have to have real *coglioni,* as Trueblood and his partners themselves put it: balls. They were *maestri del film a basso budget,* they would brag. These brazen, single-minded, self-proclaimed masters of low-budget horror movies would make a film in hell if they could save a lira.

Stephen wanted to close his eyes and sleep; he needed a sharp mind for what lay ahead. But at the same time, he did not dare drop his guard, not for a moment, especially when Colon was present. He'd been warned.

"When you arrive in Bel-*grad*-o, pay att*en*tion," a secretary ("Assistant to the Producer," as she preferred to be called) told him in a call from Rome. She spoke with a heavy Italian accent, stressing the second syllables. "Watch out es*pec*ially for the line pro*du*cer, Co*lon*," she said, and added in a hissing whisper: "He is a *snake.*"

– 5 –

The Hotel Obrenović was one of the oldest hotels operating in Yugoslavia. Colon had selected it because of its location on the Terazije square in the heated core of Belgrade's downtown, at the confluence of the Sava and Danube rivers. Everything they would need for studio shooting was nearby. Avala Studios Beôgrad was thirty minutes away.

With a click Stephen entered his room. It was even more spartan than he expected. Supposedly this was a 4-star hotel, or so Colon had informed him on the drive into the city. "Cost us what a Motel Six charges in the States," Colon had boasted. The walls had cracks in them. The sink's drain had rust at the edges. He tried the faucet. The water that spurted from the tap was brownish. The shower consisted of a hole in the chipped tile floor blackened by mildew and a handheld sprayer on the end of a flexible cable dangling from the wall like a flaccid octopus tentacle. No shower curtains. The furniture was old, musty, utilitarian. According to Colon, if he was to be believed, Kirk Douglas had stayed in this room while he was shooting *Scalawag,* a 1973 movie he'd directed and starred in. Douglas chose Belgrade for the production headquarters of his movie, Colon claimed, partly because he was friends with Yugoslavian president Josip Broz Tito.

It was 10:35 p.m. Belgrade time, and Stephen was tired; it had been a long trip, and he could not sleep on the flight. Work on the film would begin the next day at 6:00 a.m.; he would set his alarm for 5. He wanted to call Elaine to reassure her that he would be sacrificing all creature comforts to make this film; that he felt miserable without her; that he missed her and their daughter to death; that she shouldn't worry, he'd be okay. He wanted to talk to little Em. He wanted to tell her he loved her with all his heart. But he decided that he would get some sleep first, then make the call. When he spoke to his wife, he hoped to sound strong, clear-headed—capable.

He lay down on the narrow bed. He needed to wake up feeling prepared for the day. He would finally rest …

– 6 –

He awoke suddenly, disoriented. He looked at his watch resting on the tiny bedside table. It was 1:37 a.m. local time.

He hurried downstairs, four flights—the elevator was broken—and entered one of three vintage phone booths in the lobby, a box like an upright coffin made of mahogany, the varnish long gone. He stared at the phone. The concierge had explained how to use it when he first arrived.

"Medugradski razgovor?" Long distance talk? "Will take few minutes," warned the clerk, whose ghostly white complexion suggested he never left the confines of the hotel.

Stephen had a pocketful of dinars. He'd exchanged his dollars for the local currency at the airport. His $300 weekly per diem, which he would receive each Monday, would translate into thousands of banknotes: about 10,000 Yugoslav dinars equaled one U.S. dollar. (A 2,000,000-dinar bill was introduced in 1989 as a result of the hyperinflation, but it wasn't available yet. By the end of that year, inflation would reach 1,000 percent.) He'd pay for the call with his wife's credit card, which they had on file.

"You pay after. I gon-nect you now," explained the clerk. "You give number."

While Stephen anxiously waited for the call to be put through, he thought the gulf between himself and home was as desolate and sad as Hades—even though the home he'd left behind was foundering on the brink of ruin. His wife was as yet unaware of the affair.

The morning he left Los Angeles, Stephen kissed Elaine on the temple and whispered that he loved her. She was still half asleep and made a muffled gurgling sound in response. He'd hesitated before kissing her. She was exhausted from dealing with too much paperwork the day before at the office and desperately needed her sleep. She had a big week ahead of her. Unlike Stephen, ever the dreamer, she had a pragmatic view of most things. Someone in this family had to remain levelheaded.

What's more, she hated unnecessary drama, and his leaving would break her heart. With this new project, her husband would be gone for weeks, maybe months, and she would be alone with Emily, her four-year-old daughter from a previous marriage, left to contend with the unsentimental realities of motherhood and her job as director of the Little Ducklings preschool office. No point in shedding tears, she reasoned. No need for melodramatic goodbyes. In these situations, she preferred the surgeon's mind-set: perform a lightning-fast hatchet amputation of a gangrenous limb rather than go through endless deliberations among doctors and family members, a nauseating regimen of antibiotics, and a drawn-out recuperation period leading to a nebulous outcome. Stephen was leaving. So … just hack it off and be done with it.

After slipping silently out of their bedroom and making his way down the hall on the balls of his feet, quietly so as not to disrupt the delicate hush in their apartment, Stephen entered his stepdaughter, Emily's, bedroom. He approached the little bed in the corner, bent over and kissed her on the forehead, just below the halo of blonde curls, as she lay fast asleep, bundled snugly under the covers, dreaming of wild things and sleepy moons.

Emily opened her eyes, blinked, was awake. She looked up at Stephen.

"Daddy?"

"Sweets."

"Are you going away now?" She sat up and rubbed away the sleep in her eyes with the backs of her hands.

"For a little while," he said, whispering as he tapped his lips with a finger.

She laid a cheek against his chest and he held her in his arms. "I wish you could stay forever," she said, whispering too.

"When I get back," he began, then corrected himself: "When I come home I will stay forever." She nodded, still nestled against him. "Don't forget! You have Big Bird." He reached over to the pillow and picked up a doll propped against it. It was a stuffed, yellow, anthropomorphic canary, a character from *Sesame Street*. He placed the doll in her waiting hands. "When you feel sad or lonely, you know Big Bird will be there for you."

She pulled away from Stephen and hugged the doll to her chest. Stephen stood.

"I promise you, Em," he said, kissing the top of the child's head. It smelled of flowers, he noted—was it lavender? "You will be safe, and I will be home before you know it." The airport shuttle was due to arrive any minute. He would wait for it outside. He left Emily's room silently, waving and smiling at her encouragingly as he went.

As he stepped out of their apartment bearing a suitcase, he turned to look at the front door. He checked the lock. He was satisfied that the door was secure and his family safe. He then made his way down the stairway leading to the sidewalk.

He tried not to look back a second time but failed.

The call finally went through. Elaine answered:

"Hello?"

"Ellie! It's me."

"Stephen? Are you there?" Her voice sounded nasal. She had a cold and was weary.

He told her he was indeed there, and she sounded genuinely relieved. He told her about the hotel, about Colon, about the long flight. He left out the part about the airport police.

"What time is it at home?" he asked.

"Almost five. I'm about to prepare Em some dinner. Her favorite, mac 'n' cheese."

Then a staticky voice— *"EL-LO? EL-LO? EX-CUSE ME?"* A woman's husky, Slavic-accented voice came on the line. Stephen was confused.

"What? Who is this?" said Stephen, gripping the phone tightly in his hand.

"ZA POLICIJU. YOU–MUST–SPEAK–SLOW."

"Who is that woman, Stephen? What's going on?" Elaine asked, alarmed.

Then Stephen remembered. Colon had explained when they arrived at the hotel.

"Sorry, sweetheart. It's the Belgrade police. She's translating. They're monitoring the call."

"Are you kidding me?"

"No, I'm not kidding, sweetheart. I'm in Yugoslavia."

"SLOW PLEASE!"

"Stephen. The police? This isn't funny. I'm worried."

"Ellie, really. You don't have to worry."

"Well, I *am* worried," she said with a small laugh.

"I'm okay. It's fantastic here. Well, maybe not fantastic." He caught himself. He was supposed to be working hard while his wife worked her full-time job as director of Little Ducklings Daycare and cared for a four-year-old. He must not appear to be having a good time. "The hotel's pretty crappy." Then: "Can I talk to Em?"

"Wait. She just ran out of the kitchen. Hold on …"

Stephen looked at his watch. He would report to work

at six o'clock, in about four hours. He hoped adrenalin would see him through the day. A minute later, he heard the rattling of the phone as his wife came back on the line. Her voice sounded staticky:

"Stephen—? ... You–u ther—ere?"

"I'm here."

"She ran to her room."

"What?"—shocked.

"She ran off."

"Em didn't want to talk to me?" asked Stephen dolefully.

"It's not that. Please, sweetheart. Don't take it person-ally. Hey, you know, she's only a *kid*," she said, as if she needed to jog his memory after the long trip. "Look. I think maybe she misses you *too much* to talk. That's what it is. I'm sure that's it. It's just, well ... she's *sad*."

Which was not what he wanted to hear. He did not want Emily or his wife to feel badly on his account. It only made the experience of being so thoroughly displaced more painful.

"It might also be she doesn't know how to act," she went on, and reminded him once more, more emphatically: "She's *four*."

Her words only left him feeling bruised.

"Oh, Stephen ..." She spoke gently now, in the only manner she could think of to mollify him. Her voice sounded so sweet, so reassuring, so—

That's when it hit him. Stephen missed his little family already and he'd only just arrived. That's how quickly Belgrade had its effect: adrift on a dark sea, treading water—or slowly drowning. Time would tell which.

— 7 —

He couldn't sleep. It was a strange bed in a strange land. His thoughts ran wild. He'd made so many mistakes. He'd blundered outrageously by having the affair. He should have confessed, asked for Elaine's forgiveness, somehow fallen to his knees. Why had he acted so foolishly?

Diane Barnes (a stage name; née Diefenbach), his ill-fated paramour, stepped into Stephen's life at an opportune moment. She had a job answering phones at a small talent agency on Sunset Boulevard on the West Side; she hoped to make it as an actress someday, and the job placed her in the web of the film industry. Stephen was there to drop off his director's reel. There was an instant connection when they saw each other. Stephen had trouble taking his eyes off her: she was beautiful, in her way. He hadn't seen it at first, then he did. Her natural honey-blonde hair was a rare sight in this city of Debbie Harry–bleached blondes; she wore it loose and kept stroking it. Her flawless complexion seemed to glow with a light from within.

They talked. She asked about his reel. He told her he

was a screenwriter and director. He described his movie *Sucker* to her. She was impressed. From her perspective as an actress, he represented a possible acting job. He might, someday, be the next John Hughes. He was married—she saw right away the wedding ring on his finger—but that did not matter. This was Hollywood. As far as Stephen could tell, an "all's-fair-in-love-and-war" philosophy seemed to prevail. And here was this young woman—21, 22 maybe?— chatty, vivacious, electrified, and electrifying. Stephen was enchanted.

He left the demo reel on her desk. They continued their conversation at the Cat & Fiddle Pub on Highland.

"The one thing we can never get enough of is love," she told him brightly over a Dos Equis, "and the one thing we never *give* enough is love"—from Henry Miller, one of her many heroes. "Live in the moment, for the *brightest* of moments," she said, unfurling her radiant smile.

Stephen saw no reason to disagree with this uplifting philosophy, at least theoretically; these were dark times. The scripts weren't selling. He was two months behind on the rent. His Sears and Wells Fargo credit cards had been canceled. Elaine worked long hours and, since they shared a car and she took it to work every day, he was marooned at home much of the time. There was far too little bright- ness in Stephen's life. This woman was as bright as freshly minted silver dollars.

They had several beers that afternoon. Then they left the pub and she showed him her apartment in West Hollywood, near Third and Fairfax. This was before she moved to the

Venice apartment, which was smaller and more expensive but close to the beach, where she would enjoy roller-skating in her short shorts and oversized sunglasses, sipping a smoothie on the crowded, frenetic Venice Boardwalk.

As puerile as all this sounds—she had a longtime boyfriend, a relationship as serious as Stephen and Elaine's—their affair ("covenant," as she preferred to call it) was thrilling and suited her nonconformist Wiccan philosophy. She preferred that Stephen refer to her not as a "feminist," a term that carried all kinds of "negative baggage," she felt, but as a "witch"—a charged word, to be sure, but in her mind a benign one to be used reverentially. She insisted that she was not the kind of witch that boiled babies' entrails and eyes of newts in bubbling cauldrons. Rather, she cast spells that involved healing, love, harmony, wisdom, and creativity. Her potions cured headaches and caused people to fall in love. (She'd later cast several spells on Stephen, but without success.) She indulged in all-natural remedies ("No preservatives, ever!") such as rosemary, thyme, and lavender, when confronted with psychic disturbances ranging from black auras to erectile dysfunction. ("Don't worry, sweetheart, mint can create a lovemaking adventure," she bubbled supportively during one particularly discouraging tryst.) And because Diane's views on love were more pagan than Christian and were thus unconstrained by any notion of sin; because Stephen found their encounters wildly exciting, temporarily lifting him out of his depression; because her bewitching beauty was impossible to ignore—Stephen succumbed to his desires.

Diane was aware of his weaknesses; he was a man, after all. She silently cultivated a belief that with a strict devotion to her religious faith, she would ultimately heal Stephen of his "Wounds of Patriarchy," as she put it. Men like Stephen were victims of not only their own debilitating biology, but of a decaying culture that undervalued women's spiritual powers. He wasn't a "sexist pig," she claimed, an ad hominem expression used at the time by the more radical wing of the feminist movement that she found overly reductive. He was merely a victim of his own biology. "Love the man, hate the biology" was her motto; she had a bumper sticker on her car advertising this maxim. Men were slaves to testosterone and their Stone Age habits, she genuinely believed, all of them Stanley Kowalskis. Goddess Power would liberate them, help them recognize and fall in love with women's inner beauty and goodness. With persistence and the right mixture of spells, Stephen would eventually throw off his slavish chauvinist chains, leave his wife, and move in with her.

Maybe someday he'd even put her in one of his movies.

– 8 –

A knock at the door woke Stephen. He looked at his watch. It was 5:20. He'd overslept, having forgotten to set his portable wind-up clock, which he'd left in his suitcase propped against a wall. He was already late. First day, no less.

"Mister Stephen. *Mister Stephen!* Car is leaving five thirty," came the disembodied voice.

Still disheveled and dressed in the previous day's clothes, Stephen opened the door. A young man stared at him. He reminded Stephen of Johnny Rotten but with lots of wild black hair; pale, almost translucent white skin in stark contrast to the hair. He was shifting his weight from one leg to the other with nervous energy, back and forth, like a boxer. He appeared electrified by life's opportunities.

"Mr. Stephen? Are you American director?" he asked.

"I am."

"Oh. Good. Is correct room. I am Zivko."

"Zivko," Stephen echoed, trying out the Serbian accent. "You must be the driver."

"Driver? Yes. Is trans-por-ta-tion," he said carefully. "Foot soldier, more like it. I go anywhere. Get anything. *Do* anything." He raised an eyebrow cunningly.

Stephen was not sure how to respond. He stood there, waiting stupidly.

"I wait out front," said Zivko.

After he quickly showered and dressed—leather cowboy boots with sharp pointed toes meant for stirrups, Levi's jeans, thick gray wool sweater—Stephen glanced at his reflection in the bathroom mirror. He looked tolerably decent, despite the bags under his eyes. He displayed the early stages of a full beard that he believed would bolster his legitimacy as a film director. Scorsese, Coppola, Spielberg—they all had beards.

He reached into his suitcase and snapped up his notebook with all his production notes and sketches, as well as the latest version of the script. He scooped up his passport and wallet from the bedside table, jammed them into his pants pockets. He then locked the door behind him as he left the room.

He'd wanted to call Elaine, but there was no time. His heart ached for her, but he had a job to do. As he thought about the day ahead, a growing excitement began to replace the melancholy.

He felt like an *agent provocateur.* As a double agent in Belgrade, working on an international movie production, he would have to navigate one side—that of Truth and Loyalty—and then the other—that of Mendacity and Betrayal. He feared the potential defections.

– 9 –

The trip to Avala Studios was a half-hour's drive.

"I brought you breakfast, you will like, I think," Zivko said as he reached behind the seat with his right hand, his left still clutching the steering wheel, momentarily teetering precariously between the front and back seats, gaze glued to the road ahead, scaring the hell out of Stephen.

"Watch out! What're you doing?"

Zivko dug up a brown paper bag from the floor behind his seat and handed it to Stephen. "Is *gibanica*."

"What?"

"Egg and cheese pie."

Stephen opened the bag and slid out a small Styrofoam container. "Thanks," he said, relieved although as yet unsure what to expect. There would be no time to stop for breakfast, so he'd eat whatever it was. Turned out it would be the first of many egg dishes he'd consume in the coming weeks. As Stephen ate the buttery pastry, actually quite tasty, melted cheese and scrambled egg, yellow crumbs quickly blanketed his lap like a fresh winter's snowfall. Zivko drove the streets wildly—like Cary Grant in the drunk-driving scene in Hitchcock's *North by Northwest,* recalled Stephen. The car was a junker and rattled alarmingly at every corner. Zivko made sudden turns.

"You know where you're going?" asked Stephen, tightly gripping the tiny leather support strap that hung from the ceiling.

"Yes. Studio. I think maybe late."

Stephen tensed. He wanted everything to go smoothly. Colon would be in full raptor mode, ready to strike. He'd better be on time.

"They shoot *Around World in Eight Days.* Right here."

"Eighty." Stephen gritted his teeth as the car made an unexpected hard turn.

"Yeah. Eighty. Is TV show? You know Peace Brose Man?"

Stephen smiled. He quickly rewired his brain to think like Zivko.

"You mean Pierce Brosnan?"

"That's it! Beeeg star! You know him? Was right fooking here."

"No kidding. Remington Steele himself. In Belgrade!" said Stephen, mostly to himself, shaking his head, impressed.

Stephen thought about the cast for his movie. Few Americans were familiar with—or they had long forgotten—the true talent of their ostensible "star," Kurt Buckfellow, who'd worked for some of the biggest *auteurs* of the American New Wave of the sixties. He'd made brief appearances in such classics as *Bonnie and Clyde, The Graduate, The Wild*

Bunch, and *Easy Rider* (as an extra). In the seventies, he'd costarred in or played a guest role on a number of TV shows, mostly westerns: *Alias Smith and Jones* and the long-running *Little House on the Prairie* displayed his best work. He'd collaborated with many action movie stars: Stallone, Bronson, Willis—all the big names. But in the eighties, he'd acquired massive gambling debt. He also had blistering alimony payments to make to his ex-wife. To survive, he resorted to taking lesser parts in low-budget action and horror films to pay the mounting bills. And then it became a Catch-22 predicament: the more he fell into debt, the more bad movies he signed on for; the more he gained the reputation as a B-movie actor, the more the big studios shunned him; the more desperate he became, the more he gambled to stay solvent. The producers in Rome knew how to exploit men like Buckfellow; they knew how to market his name all over the world. They would bleed him until he was dead. In the meantime, Stephen, as his director, would have to palliate his wounded ego and extract a decent performance from him.

"Coffee?" asked the young driver, turning to look at Stephen, who appeared downcast.

"When I get to the studio. Just drive, please."

Stephen studied the driver, who was now avidly watching the road ahead as he increased speed. Big hair, punk, New Wave, and Communism, all rolled up into one. Stephen felt like he'd passed through Lewis Carroll's looking glass.

"You okay?" said Zivko, now staring at Stephen.

"I'm fine," he replied. He shifted in the seat, turning

away uncomfortably from the young man's persistent gaze. "Watch the road!" he shouted suddenly.

The driver of a car coming in the opposite direction blasted his horn. Zivko lurched back into his lane. Stephen closed his eyes. He felt dizzy. After a long period during which a tense hush fell over them, Stephen broke the silence:

"That was close."

"Yes. Close call. Just about ended whole movie production right there."

"Please be careful."

Zivko gripped the wheel tighter with both hands and stared fixedly at the road ahead.

Stephen turned and looked ahead toward a great fortress of hills, calming himself. Then: "What did you mean back there? That you can get me anything. Like what?"

"Yes, is true," said the young man, brightening. "What you need? Shaver? Game Boy? Etch A Sketch?"

Stephen thought for a moment. Was he a dealer on the black market? Was he dangerous? A lunatic? Against his better judgment, Stephen asked, "Can you get me a VCR?"

"VCR? What is VCR?"

Was Yugoslavia still in the Ice Age? thought Stephen.

"Video cassette recorder. To play movies. I'd like to be able to watch something in my room at night." Stephen realized how ridiculous this might sound, considering his brutal production schedule. "For inspiration," he added lamely.

"Oh, sure! VCR easy. Next day. Really *chip*."

"Wait a second. Do they even have something like a Blockbuster in Belgrade?"

"What is Blockbuster?"

"A video store. They're big in the U.S," explained Stephen, although the chain had only been around since 1985.

"Ah! YE YE Videoz, on Knez Mihailova. Is main shopping place in Beôgrad."

Stephen thought about this. When would he have free time to watch videos? To go shopping, of all things. He looked out the window forlornly. Hungarian and Turkey oaks dotted the landscape. They soon drove past a large concrete structure with five gigantic concrete fins combined to create a star.

"What's that?" asked Stephen, pointing at it.

"Kosmaj monument. Is to honor who dies in the National Liberation Struggle. Was back in Second World War."

"Impressive."

"Yes, im-pres-seeve!" Zivko said brightly. The young man looked at Stephen, then at the road ahead, and then back at Stephen. "I get anything. Like I say. Skunk? Coke? You name it. I am regular one-man phar-ma-ceu-ti-cal company," he said proudly, having mastered a difficult multisyllabic English word. Belgrade had become the center of smugglers, dealers, and addicts. "Serbia is the Colombia of Europe," Colon would later explain. "Heroin from Kosovo, which you can get for a thousand dinar a gram, if your heart so desires." It was popular with high society clients—heads of state, celebrity film stars, and big-shot directors like Stephen.

Stephen sighed. He'd had little experience with drugs—a joint at a party years ago, snorting coke once in college. This talk of illicit drugs made him feel uneasy. He was in a foreign country—a Communist one, no less.

He immediately thought of home, how safe he always felt there, although Santa Monica was a relatively big city. Kitchen, living room, bathroom, two bedrooms—the length, width and breath of his home. The parameters of peace.

He then tried to envision the unknowable future, to remain optimistic.

But his own demons whispered distractingly in his ear.

– 10 –

Located on a forested hill above the Yugoslavian capital, Avala Studios came at one-quarter the cost of Rome's Cinecittà. It was a complex of facilities located in the heart of a large park, six kilometers away from Stephen's hotel: four sound stages, offices, vehicle storage, water tank. Studios 1, 5, and 7 were used for TV shows. (*Velo Misto* was a particular local favorite at that time. Although the story had numerous subplots and dozens of different characters, the focus of the show was given to Hajduk, the world-famous soccer club.) The other studios were reserved for movies.

Some members of the local crew were willing to work for 1,189 Yugoslavian dinars per day; the same went for background extras (actors without speaking parts—"human props," Colon liked to say). This was an amount equivalent to one U.S. dollar. With the nine hundred thousand dollars budgeted for the film, they could make an epic with a cast of thousands. They could make something magnificent and lasting, Stephen imagined—if they chose to.

He could already imagine the poster, although he had

not shot a single foot of film stock yet. His name and the new title—a title he dreamed up himself; he worried, though, that some people might not know what it meant—were emblazoned across the top of the poster, above the image of a limp, pallid woman with two raw, bloody fang holes in her neck:

INFERNAL BEAUTY
A FILM BY
STEPHEN CRAWFORD

Crawford would suit him better. Krawczyk sounded too foreign, and he was tired of having to spell it for people. The "czy" in his name confused people. He hoped to separate himself forever from the clunky surname, which had begun to feel like an extra limb—a burdensome, withered third arm. Why hadn't his grandfather chosen a nice, easy-to-spell, Anglicized name when he arrived at Ellis Island, like most of the immigrants from Eastern Europe? He would file with Social Security for a name change as soon as he got back to the States. *Crawford*. It had a nice classic movie ring to it. Joan Crawford. Broderick Crawford. He wished his name was as romantic sounding as, say, William Holden or Montgomery Clift. No. He would make do; it would have to be Stephen *Crawford*. Elaine would just have to make the adjustment.

The first production meeting took place in one of the larger meeting rooms. Stephen sat on a lime-green couch facing a crescent of about twenty men and women sitting in stiff, white plastic chairs.

"Have they worked with Americans?" Stephen asked

Colon, who had just walked into the room like he owned it.

"This is Yugoslavia, not Siberia," he said derisively.

Colon paced back and forth like Julius Caesar before his legions at Gaul. He waited until they had stopped talking and he had their full attention.

"People," he intoned officiously. He swiveled his eyes around the room with reptilian coldness.

The translators went to work, speaking as unobtrusively as they could:

"Persone!"

"Svijet!"

"This man here is Mr. Krawczyk," Colon said, pointing an accusing finger at Stephen, who winced at the sound of his name. He never could get used to the foreign reverberations. It sounded to him like another species. Like Crawfish. "He will be your new *director.*" He said the word director like it meant something grand, worthy of respect. *Not me, surely,* thought Stephen. *Travis Bickle: You talkin' to me?*

"Stephen Crawford!" erupted Stephen suddenly, sounding like he'd sneezed violently. It was a mistake. He knew it the moment he spoke. Colon stared at him like he'd lost his mind. "Please call me Stephen," he said quietly, opening his palms heavenward in supplication.

Everyone looked questioningly at the new director. They were confused. None of them was sure what he meant by his request; this behavior was something new. Was it an act of humility? Of excessive pride? Of madness? But then, this man was an American; that might explain the peculiarities, the unorthodoxy. Moreover, generally speaking, American directors were as rare a sight in Belgrade as anteaters. That said, this was the reality: Stephen would be their leader during the weeks ahead—Colon made that clear. Hopefully the man was sane.

Stephen simply wanted to be looked upon as one of the team. Colon had his own ideas, however: "He will be your *god* for the next three weeks," he announced, responding to their perplexed expressions, intending to repair the damage of Stephen's outburst. "You will make Mr. Krawczyk's job as easy as possible"—a declarative statement. No requesting.

"*Vaš director,*" said a man with a long face white as paper and a thin black mustache. He was the production's official Serbian translator. He instructed the crew: "*Učinit ćeš njegov posao što je moguće lakšim.*" You will make his job easy. He then turned to Stephen expectantly.

"*Mister Krawczyk,*" said Colon sternly, ignoring the Yugoslavian man with the long pale face, facing Stephen foursquare now. "You will have two translators during the production meetings. One Yugoslavian, one Italian. *This* man …" he said, bending a thumb like a hitchhiker in the direction of the Italian translator, who was built like a wrestling coach rather than a linguist: squat and ready for a match, "… is from Rome. Some of the Italians speak English, but they don't speak a jot of Serb. And vice versa."

It would be difficult enough to make this movie with an all-English-speaking crew, figured Stephen. He feigned calm, but inside he sensed butterflies stirring.

Colon walked over to another man who was standing

at the back of the room. This new person was tall, burly, and heavily muscled. ("Built like a Slav," Colon would say condescendingly.) He was also bald as a tea kettle.

"He is Borko," said Colon. "Our first unit production manager. Basically, he will take care of everything."

The big man smiled politely and extended his hand to Stephen. "Good to meet you, Mr. Stephen. I look forward to working with you." The man had heard his first-name-only request a moment ago and honored it, more or less; Stephen was delighted.

"Likewise," he said, and Borko smiled warmly as they shook hands. "I have to say, Borko. You sound like a native Californian." He realized as soon as he said it that the statement was meaningless. What was "Californian," after all? People there were from all over. The Bronx. Appalachia. Texas. Ohio. There were Latinos in Boyle Heights. Valley girls in Studio City. Surfers in Huntington Beach. Black folks, white folks, Asians, Native Americans … *Eh, watcha! Sup, aye? Oh my gawd! Fer shure! Yo, dude! Rad barrels out there, man! Far out.* A veritable Tower of Babel. "Your accent, I mean," Stephen added. "Or lack of it, I guess."

"I matriculated from one of your great universities. USC Film School? You know of it?" he said with a wink. The man spoke English as smooth as butter.

"George Lucas studied there," replied Stephen.

"Well, actually, I studied under one of the world's great *cinematographers*: Slavko Vorkapić."

Stephen looked hard at Borko. He did not know the

filmmaker, but he was impressed. A cinematographer who was esteemed enough to teach at the University of Southern California—that was something.

"But his best work, I think, was this thing called kinetic editing. You've seen it, I am sure of it. *Dr. Jekyll and Mr. Hyde? David Copperfield? The Good Earth? Mr. Smith Goes to Washington?* Little movies like that. He cut them all!"—the trademark Borko smile beamed.

"Crazy," was all Stephen could say. Words were inadequate to express his admiration. The man before him had rubbed shoulders with a filmmaker who had actual linkage to Hollywood's Golden Age. Here was something to celebrate, something to venerate.

"And what in the name of Sam Hell am I doing here in Belgrade, you may ask?" he said, dramatically throwing his hands up into the air in consternation. "Why on God's green earth am I not making movies in Hollywood? The answer should be obvious, I think. I am helping you to make a masterpiece!" With Borko, everything had to be theatrical, ostentatious, bigger than life. Every sentence was an exclamation. It was a mannerism befitting a dramatic medium, the movies—especially the horror genre.

"Appreciate it," said Stephen simply.

The big man turned and made a sweeping gesture indicating the crew. "We await your orders, Captain Ahab."

"Right. Okay." Stephen cleared his throat. "Thanks, Starbuck," playing along. He glanced over at Colon, who was frowning disapprovingly. Stephen then turned and smiled nervously at the group. It was with an awareness of his own rawness that he said to them, with as much humility he could muster, "I'd like to thank all of you."

While he spoke, the translators did their best to follow along, sounding like two radios tuned to different stations in the background. Stephen explained that he liked to begin movie productions—he'd done it at the outset of both his short films—with a prayer. He was not particularly religious; in fact, he hadn't visited a church since he was a little boy. *Movies* were his religion. He enjoyed the sense of community in a film crew or the spectators nestled together in dark movie theaters—his generation's churches—taking part in the sacredness of all Art.

He bowed his head. The others looked at each other, unsure of how to respond, then followed his lead.

"Bless this crew," he began. There were looks of confusion. Some rolled their eyes. A few smirks. Colon was still frowning, his ruddy skin growing redder by the moment. The translations continued:

"Blagoslovi ovu posadu ..."

"Benedici questo equipaggio ..."

Stephen said he was grateful for the talent they offered, for the opportunity to make this film, for the artists' muses, for the new day, for the goodness of life itself. He wished them well on their new jobs. When he finished speaking, some of the crew actually made the sign of the cross.

He huddled with Borko in a corner of the room. He showed Borko his notebook with sketches of the boarding school.

He wanted an otherworldly, Grimm Brothers fairy tale look. Something creepy. He asked Borko if there were schools here that fit the description.

"Like this?" he said, studying Stephen's drawings. "Ha! Ha!" he chuckled. "Not this side of Transylvania, I'm afraid."

They would *build* the exterior, the big man explained, to his specifications, the exterior on location, and the interiors at Avala. They had the money for sets, which were generally cheaper than shooting on location. Shipping the crew and equipment all over Belgrade was time consuming and costly. On a set they could move the walls, do whatever they wanted.

"We can destroy it. Set it on fire, if you wish," Borko said impishly, eyes twinkling. "Blow it up!"

Stephen smiled. He knew immediately that he could work with this man.

"We need a scary forest around the school too," Stephen added, impassioned. "Misty, black, rotting trees. The feeling of death and decay everywhere …"

"I'll put the location coordinator on it. We will find you death and decay."

"And a cave," added Stephen.

"Cave?" he repeated, taken aback. "What kind of cave?"

Hasn't he read the script? wondered Stephen. It was a big scene. The vampires would rise from their earthen beds in a murky, cavernous domain, a lowest level of Dante's *Inferno.* "A vast underworld. *Really* big," said Stephen. "And bat-filled. Millions of them. Real, if possible. Not rubber bats—*real* bats." (Computer-generated imagery wouldn't be in wide use until years later, in the 90s.)

"What? No cheap Bela Lugosi special effects?" Borko asked in mock surprise.

Stephen smiled. This would be fun after all.

"Okay," said Borko. "The one you want is Resava Cave, the biggest system in all of Yugoslavia ..." He paused, thinking. "Never mind. Maybe Mirijevska Cave is better."

"Good. We'll take a look," said Stephen, taking a deep breath and letting it out, relieved.

"I will get you a visa if we need it."

"A visa? What for? Where're we going?"

"Romania, Bulgaria, who knows? Better to have it. They have caves, *big* time."

Romania. The ruthless dictator Ceaușescu. The name sent a chill to the bone.

"Yes. It will all get sorted out, I think," claimed his production manager reassuringly. Borko broke into another exaggerated smile, which had the effect of temporarily easing Stephen's fears.

Borko then introduced Stephen to the art and costume department heads. He would meet later with the cinematographer, who would arrive from Rome in the morning. All was going well. But then:

"Mister Krawczyk!"—an angry voice, shouting, making Stephen jump.

He turned. It was Colon, looking pissed. Stephen was startled by his loud command.

"You will join our production manager here, Borko,"

commanded Colon. "He will take you to dinner. That way you can continue to work." And he added for good measure: "You will enjoy your meal, of course."

The ride back to the city passed quickly. Zivko at the wheel, Stephen in the passenger seat, and Borko in the back—a trinitarian configuration that would become routine. Stephen watched the road, mind adrift. Despite the fact that things were happening at a brisk pace, Stephen's mood went suddenly dark. It often happened when things started going his way. His mind pestered him: *You will botch this.* There were many good people assigned to this production, he reminded himself, hoping to mitigate his anxiety—all of them talented, dedicated people. They had the resources they'd need to make this movie. This was what he wanted, wasn't it?

Then he reminded himself: "Great men are not born great, they grow great." Vito Corleone had said the line in *The Godfather.* Brando's husky voice, cheeks stuffed with cotton. But as he thought about Coppola's body of work, Stephen's mood grew even darker still. He could never achieve that level of greatness.

He'd lost his bearings, lost confidence—but only for the briefest of moments. The lights of Kneza Mihailova—Prince Michael Street—shone brightly ahead in the otherwise darkened city, like some kind of North Star.

– 11 –

As they walked along Prince Michael Street, Stephen considered what he and Borko must look like to passersby: Lenny and George from the 1939 film *Of Mice and Men,* he thought. Borko was so much bigger, the Lon Chaney, Jr. of the two: a quintessential mesomorph with broad shoulders and narrow waist. His face was strong and intelligent, however, unlike Lenny's.

Stephen, conversely, had Burgess Meredith's more modest body type. He'd inherited his Polish grandfather's modest frame. But his western clothes, the jeans and cowboy boots, were a dead giveaway. Here, in Yugoslavia, he felt like the Ugly American next to the Mighty Slav.

Borko seemed just as enthralled with his surroundings as Stephen.

"Two years after the assassination of Prince Mihailo Obrenović in eighteen seventy, the city named it *Ulica Kneza Mihaila,*" he explained, looking at everything as if it were all new, with fresh excitement.

"Beautiful!" said Stephen. In the evening the shop lights

spilled onto the promenade and lent an enchanted air to the already exotic place.

"Yes. It is a beautiful street. A beautiful *city*, really. You will see." He broke into his habitual broad smile as he conjured up a jewel of memory. "And did you know? Prince Michael Street is included on the list of *Spatial Cultural Historical Units of Great Importance!*"—stated with beaming pride.

The latest western merchandise behind the glass storefront windows shone golden and silver. Lamps, beds, electric blenders—contemporary Ali Baba treasure strikingly incongruous with the architecture of the buildings, which was a haphazard blend of Romantic, Renaissance, and Balkan styles. It was as if Borko had said "Open sesame!" and the famous street had appeared. The street was paved with black granite slabs from Jablanica. A drinking fountain was made of white marble from Venčac. A row of oak trees running down the middle had also recently been introduced. Everywhere vintage-looking candelabra, made to resemble old gas lights, rested atop poles standing like exclamation marks. And there was a constant buzz of locals and tourists. The pedestrians lined the street, peering into the store windows in a kind of wonder.

Stephen stopped, looked around.

"Wait a second," he said. Something was amiss.

Borko followed his line of vision to a chandelier store. The crystal refracted the sparkling store lights.

"There's nobody inside," Stephen observed, incredulous. He looked at the other storefronts. "There's no one in *any* of the stores. What's the deal? The promenade is packed."

"Yes, this is true. They are here to check out the latest products from Germany, France, the U.S. But mind you, you must understand the way it is here. Most people can't afford the merchandise they see. They are, what's the expression?—window shopping?"

As they continued down the boulevard, they came to a café that was, unlike the other businesses on the street, packed to the walls with young patrons, drinking coffee and engaged in animated conversation.

"At least the café is busy," Stephen said, stopping to stare at the hectic spectacle.

"Well, why not? They buy a coffee and they can talk for hours."

"Who are these people?"

"Students. The Glorious Youth of Beôgrad, the future of our city," said Borko, his face now serious. "They are talking revolution."

The music of revolt from Stephen's youth—Jefferson Airplane, Country Joe, "The Revolution Will Not Be Televised," "Street Fighting Man"—reverberated in his head as he watched the young people hobnobbing in the café.

Stephen looked closer. Kids in their twenties, many of them with long curly hair. They reminded him of his own anti–Vietnam war activities in the sixties and early seventies. He'd witnessed most of the would-be revolution at home from the sidelines. He'd attended a handful of demonstrations, even wore a black armband after the infamous Christmas bombing of Hanoi in 1972. He'd voted for McGovern. He'd listened to Tom Hayden and Jane Fonda speak at a rally at Stanford University, where the students, whipped into a frenzied state by the speakers, rioted, breaking classroom windows and overturning trash cans. He'd missed being drafted into the army; his lottery number was 298.

"So what exactly is going on, Borko?" Stephen said.

"Planning. Political debates. Violent demonstrations. They are beginning to happen more. A plunging economy, rising nationalism—it's getting, as you Americans like to say, *hairy.*"

"What are they doing about it?"

"Who? These kids? The government? The Yugoslav Communist Party held an emergency session. This happened just last October. The entire cabinet resigned!"

Stephen's eyes widened.

"The Communist Party voted to give up its power monopoly," Borko added, raising his hands and bunching up his shoulders as if in disbelief: "And this just *happened*!"

The news staggered Stephen. He felt like he was in a war zone.

"That's just great," he said. "What do we do? I mean, we have three weeks of shooting ahead."

"Do?" Borko repeated. "*Do*, you say? What do you mean *do*?! Ha! Ha! What we will *do* is make a masterpiece, my friend. I keep *telling* you!"—stated with his usual dramatic grandiosity, placing his heavy hand once again on Stephen's shoulder.

They continued walking in silence, Stephen brooding. After a while Borko turned Stephen around with one arm, politely but abruptly. A magnificent church stood across the street. It had an Eastern Orthodox cross atop the steeple.

"You are looking at Saborna Crkva Sveca Arhangela Mihaila. It is Yugoslavian Orthodox." He turned Stephen a bit more to the left. "You must see this. We will go inside."

He led Stephen around to the left side of the church, an imposing structure built in the mid-nineteenth century. Stephen looked upward as they proceeded down a flight of stone steps. The architecture adopted the standards of neoclassical churches with a baroque tower.

"You are about to enter the heart of the revolution," said Borko hammily, adopting a sinister, ghoulish look, widening his eyes and mouth.

Borko pushed open a weather-beaten wooden door and they stepped inside the church's basement. Stephen looked about. There were two dozen people, all of them he guessed in their twenties, busy at work, murmuring in small groups, typing notes, writing Cyrillic messages on a chalk board. Some of them looked up when the two men entered; one of them waved, recognizing Borko. Some stared suspiciously for a moment at the man in the denim jeans and cowboy boots, but then quickly went back to work.

"You are witnessing the heart of the insurgency," Borko said grandly. "They are bringing oxygen to the revolution," he went on, making a sweeping gesture of his arm. He took a deep breath and let it out slowly, to emphasize the breathtaking magnificence of the tableau.

Stephen watched the youth of Serbia at work. But soon, feeling like an intruder, he turned back toward the door.

Once outside, Stephen turned to Borko, who was just closing the door. "Why here, under a church?"

"Discretion, my friend," he said. "They must be careful. The slow death of Yugoslav Communism and the rise of rival nationalist movements have kept the Church on the alert. There are spies everywhere." He twisted himself, pointed to the cross above and said, "The cross up there, with three crossbeams, two horizontal and the third one slanted? We are reminded with the slanted one of the two thieves on both sides of Christ. The one on the right ascended to heaven. The other one sank to hell." Borko turned back to face the street, pulling his coat tighter around himself and added, "There is no love here between the church and state."

– 12 –

They went on, making their way across and then down the street until they came to a restaurant. It too was located in the basement of a neoclassical building off Francuska Street. There were two worlds in Belgrade, Stephen decided: the above-ground and the subterranean one. A sign outside stated in garish red neon: *Клуб књижевника* — Klub književnika.

In a shadowed cellar — only a few iridescent tulip lamps and dim electric bulbs lit the place; it reeked of cigarette smoke — a waiter sat Borko and Stephen at a small table in the eye of the maelstrom of human activity. The place was busy. A few patrons turned their heads slightly, glancing discreetly at the new arrivals.

"What's going on? Why are they looking at us?" whispered Stephen, leaning closer to his guide.

"They are wanting to see if you are someone famous."

Stephen sat up straighter in his booth seat. A waiter approached, and Borko spoke to him in Serbian. When the waiter had left, he explained:

"I've taken the liberty of ordering a bottle. A bermet from Fruška Gora. Trust me. You will like it."

Stephen could not help looking around the room.

"They keep looking at us. Who are these people?" he said.

"Who are *you*? *That* is what they want to know. They are the local beautiful people, as you say in the States. Understand: a special part of the Klub književnika's lore is its famous patrons. Politicians. Journalists. Diplomats. Famous writers too! Men like Momo Kapor, Bogdan Tirnanić, Ivo Andrić—great men, *famous* men. All the big actors come here. Ljubinka Bobic, Jovan Milicevic, Ljubisa Jovanovic, Zoran Radmilović, Olivera Katarina. There are so many. So many big big names!"

Involuntarily Stephen scanned the faces but quickly realized he wouldn't recognize any of these people.

"But it is the *Americans* they are on the lookout for. They have come before. Alfred Hitchcock. Elizabeth Taylor—movie stars," Borko said proudly. "Marlon Brando came here, if you can believe it." He looked around the room approvingly, catching the eye of a couple of the diners, who nodded to him.

"They assume you are famous American director. Word gets around. And everything about you, how should I say, *reeks* of America." He threw a glance at Stephen's cowboy boots and winked at Stephen. "Excuse me. Maybe reeks is not the right word. I mean this with no disrespect," he said earnestly. "But never mind. They don't know anything about you. It does not matter."

Stephen felt a sudden wave of embarrassment roll over him. What if they did know who he was? Perhaps they already knew his secret. He'd directed nothing. He was nobody.

"Keep in mind," Borko went on, "remember that here, this is Communist Yugoslavia. A busy meeting place for spies, you might say." He squinted and shifted his eyes side to side in a cartoonish imitation of a spy—hunched over, squinting eyes, cocking his head rapidly back and forth. "Police informants, dressed in civilian clothing, they *mingle*—is that how you say it? —*mingle* with the guests." He cupped a hand to his left ear and turned his head, scanning the room like a radio telescope trained on the Milky Way. "Listening to *vox populi.*"

The wine came. Delicious, thought Stephen. The alcohol went right to his head, as he'd had next to nothing to eat all day. He felt empty inside, lost, as if in a dream. *What am I doing here?*

"Occasionally, much to-do," said Borko. "A fist fight broke out here between Danilo Kiš and Brana Šćepanović. Hey!" he said defensively. "You shake your head. It was a *big deal,* I am telling you. It is still talked about to this day."

While they drank their wine and waited for dinner, they discussed the plans for the next day. They would investigate a few locations, meet with the cinematographer, have another production meeting. Stephen would continue to revise the script.

The waiter arrived and placed two plates in front of Stephen and Borko. On closer inspection, the food was disappointing. A thin slab of meat: steak of some sort. The vegetables appeared limp, rubbery, their colors faded.

"What is this?" asked Stephen. "I thought you said this was an expensive restaurant." He tasted a green bean and winced. "Borko. Are these canned vegetables?"

"Expensive is relative, my friend. The economy is a disaster, civil war … we can no longer get fresh produce from Ukraine. To repeat a saying I heard in the States: it is what it is."

Stephen cut off a piece of the meat and took a bite. It was tough and chewy.

"Just remember, my American friend," said Borko with an ironic smile. "You aren't here for the cuisine. Remember? You are here to—what did I say?"

"Right. Make a masterpiece," replied Stephen dutifully, cutting another piece of the steak and thrusting it into his mouth. He was hungry. "Got it."

He was tiring of the word masterpiece. He would be happy if he simply completed the film, let alone create a work of art.

He noticed what looked like a food stain on the side of his wine glass. He turned toward the waiter to ask for a fresh glass, but the man was nowhere in sight.

– 13 –

As soon as he returned to the hotel, he went straight to the front desk. He asked if there were any messages for him. There weren't. He looked around the lobby. It was empty, gloomy, and poorly lit. There was no bar in the hotel, no diversions. The small restaurant in the rear of the lobby was always empty, at least when Stephen was looking; a lone waiter, dressed in a white uniform, stood in front, waiting for the rare diner, clearly bored to death. Nothing to read on the table next to the sofa and chairs except a few Serbian magazines. Stephen told himself he must buy a book, any book written in English, tomorrow. He wondered if Zivko would succeed at scoring a VCR.

This was all distraction, of course. None of these things mattered. He had work to do. He should be revising the script. He should be sketching scenes in his notebook. He should be working until he dropped.

When he got to his room after trudging up the four flights of stairs, he was exhausted. He sniffed. What was he smelling? Dirty socks? He looked around the tiny room and it appeared just as he had left it.

He immediately felt trapped and alone.

He carefully locked the door behind him and went straight to the bathroom. There a whiff of chlorine greeted his nose. He brushed his teeth and scrubbed and scrubbed his face with coarse soap and tepid water.

He got into bed and waited for sleep. He would call Elaine in the morning, when his thinking would be clearer. He did not want to sound tired and defeated on the phone. If he called in the morning, it would be okay.

But he could not sleep; he was too wound up from the day's events and felt as if he'd had too much caffeine; he had in fact drunk several cups of strong Serbian coffee.

He crossed over to a tiny TV, an old GE with rabbit ears, and turned it on. Sitting on the edge of the bed he watched the news. The female news anchor was speaking in Serbian, leaving Stephen to puzzle out her meaning. A photograph of a bearded man wearing round spectacles dominated the frame. Underneath his picture was a name: *Salman Rushdie.* Then another bearded man, wearing a white turban, appeared alongside Rushdie. Stephen recognized him: Ayatollah Ruhollah Khomeini. Stephen struggled to decipher the anchor's meaning as she spoke over the images. One word, "Fatwa," was intelligible, displayed along the bottom of the screen. And then he noticed the date in the upper right corner: *14 Februar, 1989.* His heart skipped a beat.

It was Valentine's Day and he'd failed to call Elaine.

– 14 –

Stephen thought of San Francisco. It was where he'd met Elaine.

"Hey, Stevey," said Charlie, opening the door of his apartment in Noe Valley, a charming enclave far from the bustling Financial District downtown. The adjacent Twin Peaks partly block the coastal fog, making the neighborhood unusually sunnier and warmer than others in the city. The isolation, warm climate, and many examples of Victorian and Edwardian residential architecture in Noe Valley have long attracted those in the know. Today the likes of Mark Zuckerberg and other celebrities reside in what are now multimillion-dollar Victorians. In the eighties, however, years before the invading tech industry drove prices through the roof, recent college graduates such as Charlie Goldberg could manage the rent.

He and Stephen had been roommates in Berkeley as Cal students, living in a big but cheap house on Blake Street in the flatlands—the lower-income neighborhood that students could afford. Stephen still lived there.

Stephen had begun his studies at UC as an English major; Shakespeare, Chaucer, and Milton were core subjects. He switched majors to film history and theory during his third year, when he also took a night class at nearby Laney College in Oakland: an introductory course on editing and cinematography. He met Charlie in a UC film class entitled French New Wave and Auteur Theory. He made the short film *Sucker* in his senior year.

A young woman stood behind Charlie. She and Stephen looked at each other. Their eyes locked and they couldn't look away.

"Elaine," Charlie went on, as Stephen advanced toward her to shake her hand, "this is Stephen."

"Hello," Elaine said. Just one word, but in a voice that was deeply assured. It seemed, to Stephen's way of thinking, not to emit from her body but from the heavens.

Charlie turned to Stephen, who was still gazing at Elaine. She had the most beautiful smile he'd ever seen. She was every film goddess—Louise Brooks, Vivien Leigh, Rita Hayworth, Ava Gardner, Hedy Lamarr, Grace Kelly—every beautiful classic movie actress he'd ever admired, all rolled up into one.

Self-conscious, shy, she seemed to writhe in Stephen's gaze with small twists of her body.

"Remember Blotter Acid Davey?" said Charlie.

Stephen reluctantly broke his gawp and turned to Charlie, momentarily disoriented. But it was hopeless. He did not hear a word that Charlie spoke—he was spellbound by Elaine. He'd taken a course on the ancient Greeks. This lovely woman before him embodied the notion of Pythagorean beauty—*symmetry*. The lines of Elaine's face were perfect, balanced, harmonious. But the ancients also saw beauty as a manifestation of the divine. Stephen thought, *This woman, this Elaine—is divine.* And there was that marvelous smile to cap it off.

But it was more than a simple matter of beauty and divinity. She was the woman who was going to save him.

Then, as explanation, Charlie added in response to her questioning look: "Sorry, Elaine. Davey was our other roommate. A chemistry major. He made his own LSD. Little red dots on little squares of paper."

Stephen frequently visited his pal Charlie in the city, especially when he was hungry and his grant money from the university wasn't due for another week. There were many weeks when he subsided solely on a diet of Aunt Jemima brand rice. Charlie, however, always had food. And Stephen always managed to show up at the dinner hour, although Charlie welcomed his friend's company and never turned him away. This time when he appeared on Charlie's doorstep, his friend already had guests—Elaine and Emily.

"Well, look who's here," exclaimed Charlie, spinning around. Into the room burst a little girl with a bird's nest of wild curly blonde hair; she raced to her mother, shrieking with joy, and wrapped her arms around her legs. Bound, her mother teetered precariously from side to side.

"Oh!" said Elaine, laughing a little. "This is my daughter, Emily."

"Hi there," said Stephen, delighted. "Would you look

at that gold hair!" Elaine's hair, in striking contrast to her daughter's, was coffee black.

The little girl released her mother, who walked across the room to pick up a cup of coffee on the kitchen counter. When Elaine walked, she left Stephen weak.

"Yes," she said as she watched her daughter, who was dancing about, doing her best to imitate the moves of the dancer in *Flashdance*. "She gets that a lot." Then, added as explanation: "Her biological father." She said the word "biological" as if the child had come from a laboratory, a mad scientist's experiment gone awry.

"She's a handful, though," added Charlie, shaking his head. Elaine gave him a look, dismayed.

"She has her mother's beautiful brown eyes," said Stephen quickly. Elaine's smile returned just as Charlie's faded.

The three adults talked for an hour. Stephen and Elaine only occasionally took their eyes off each other to acknowledge something Charlie was saying. Meanwhile Emily ran around the room with excitement, enjoying chasing her invisible, imaginary friend whom she called "John."

Charlie sensed danger. He scraped the back of his neck with his fingernails nervously.

"Em's entered the terrible twos, I think," Elaine said. "A term I don't really like. More like '*rambunctious* twos.' She's so funny. She'll say something innocuous—something like, 'My shoe! My shoe!', which has just fallen off her foot—and then melodramatically throw herself on the floor, flat on her back, arms flailing, crying hysterically, beside herself with emotion. Almost always over the littlest things! I guess you could say she's been something of a drama queen." She looked at Stephen to gauge his response.

He responded, "She's a beautiful child just bursting with life, that's all. As it should be." He was not watching little Emily at that moment; he was looking at Elaine.

He looked like a man in love.

One week later Elaine called Stephen, who was writing a paper on Hitchcock for a film theory class. It was on the duality of human nature in *Psycho*. Stephen was fascinated with matters of good and evil.

"Do you want to have dinner sometime?" she asked cheerfully. "I'd like to try out a new dish on you."

He was startled. "Uh, sure. Sure! But ... how did you get my number?"

"Charlie gave it to me."

"Wait. I thought you two were a hot item." He regretted using the term "hot item," which sounded like something from the fifties, as soon as he'd said it. And somehow the word "hot" did not quite apply to a goddess.

She seemed unfazed. "We're friends. Charlie's a really nice guy, but we're just friends. He said he was fine with it."

Stephen was unconvinced. Charlie had talked about Elaine as if she were more than a friend. When later he called Charlie to clear up the matter, Charlie's voice was monotonal: "I don't care."

"You sure, Charlie? I mean, we're old buddies. I don't want to do anything to screw up our friendship."

"No, it's fine. We broke up. Do what you want."

There was a long pause as Stephen searched for the right words to leave off with his friend. Charlie spoke first:

"She's crazy," he said, digging in.

Stephen was taken aback. "Elaine? Why do you say that?"

"I say that because she agreed to go on a little trip to Puerto Vallarta with her ex. Spent two days together."

Stephen was stunned. "What?"

"That's what I said. He's a creep."

"Why would she do that? I thought they'd broken up."

"I'm telling you."

"Where was Emily?"

"With a babysitter. Elaine asked me if I'd watch her, can you fucking believe it?"

Stephen considered the accusations. "I don't know …"

Charlie railed, "Why would she want to have anything to do with that guy!"

"Come on, Charlie," said Stephen. "That's no big surprise. He's her daughter's father. She has to see him now and then, right?"

"Doesn't matter. He's crazy and she's crazy," he said, voice unusually grave. "Two crazy little peas in a crazy little pod."

"Well …" Stephen chose his words carefully: "Look. *I* think she's beautiful. She is to me, anyway."

"Listen, man. I think there's something still going on between them. I don't need this shit. *You* don't either."

"Come on, Charlie—"

"Do what you want," he interrupted. "Just fucking do what you want."

And with that, Charlie hung up.

Stephen immediately called Elaine.

He took the BART train from downtown Berkeley to Market Street in the city. From there he caught a bus that carried him west to the Haight. He got off at Ashbury. By the eighties, and even much earlier, Haight-Ashbury had lost its 1960s Summer of Love psychedelic magic and had become a tourist trap. Carrying a bottle of wine in one hand, a wilting bouquet of flowers in the other (it was an unusually hot summer in the city), and a box of See's chocolates tucked into an armpit for little Emily, he walked down Haight Street, weaving his way through the crowd on the sidewalk, and turned left on Belvedere. At the top of the hill he found her house: a two-story, candy cane–colored Victorian. He climbed the stairs leading up to the front door. Emily answered the doorbell. She opened the door slightly, peered out suspiciously, and then, once she saw who it was, slammed it in Stephen's face.

Elaine immediately reopened it. Her face was flushed with embarrassment.

"I'm so sorry, Stephen. Please don't take it personally."

"Don't worry. I do the same thing. Door-to-door salesmen are always coming to my place to hock something. Pest control, pool cleaning services, the complete set of *Encyclopedia Britannicas* ..."

She responded with another marvelous smile.

"Do you have termite infestation?" he asked in mock seriousness, and she laughed in that way of hers: blithely, life-affirmingly. "If so, I'm your man."

"You *are* my man," she replied. She opened the door wider, and Stephen entered. He gave the box of chocolates to Emily, whose frown immediately switched to a big smile.

"Uh, oh," he said, realizing he may have made a mistake. "Maybe I should have checked with you first, before giving her the chocolate."

"No, it's fine, Stephen. It's so sweet of you! She *loves* chocolate—just like her mom. I'll just have to divvy it out judiciously, on special occasions." She turned to her daughter and nodded. "Right, Em?" Em, looking downcast, dutifully handed her mother the box.

Then Stephen gave Elaine the flowers. Her smile was never more incandescent.

That night, they drank the wine and ate her wonderful stuffed Chicken Valentino, and Stephen studied, with a scientist's fervid curiosity, Elaine's beautiful face as she told him about her divorce. Her ex did not want a child, she explained. Had no interest in fatherhood. Was an "unrepentant narcissist"—her words.

They talked all night long, covering myriad domestic and scholarly topics, firing ideas back and forth like a tennis match. She'd attended San Francisco State, and had read many of the texts Stephen had studied at Cal. They discussed William Carlos Williams, her favorite poet; Dante, one of his; Plato and Aristotle—they debated which philosopher had it right—random literary subjects before finally arriving at matters of the heart. They were so excited, their sentences played leapfrog over each other—the evenness of the tennis match left behind. Then, words were inadequate and became thoughts without even the need for sweet utterance. Put simply, they seemed to think alike. They were enthralled with each other's minds as well as hearts. Stephen had never met a woman like her. *How can this be?* he asked himself, astonished. He was confused by the new feelings. Love, Stephen discovered that night, is unsettling, cataclysmic, profound—like no experience he'd had before.

Then about three in the morning—oddly, as the thought came seemingly from left field—he remembered his friend Charlie. A twinge of guilt pestered him. A soul spasm. But they continued talking, although she sensed a subtle change in his demeanor: a pensiveness perhaps, an almost imperceptible look of melancholy shadowing the eyes. And then she simply leaned forward and kissed him—lightly but ardently.

The world opened up to him. She had the power to bestow immense happiness, he realized. He could only imagine making love to her. He would be making love to an angel. No bones, no flesh, no limbs, no hard edges—nothing of earthly substance. Only ethereal wings and light.

They talked so long and were so engrossed in each other, they failed to notice the sunrise, which was when he made up his mind: with her bewitching dark eyes and hair, she would be Beatrice to his Dante.

But there was that gnawing problem of Charlie. Stephen

would lose a friend. He tried to console himself with the line in Horace's Odes, from his Classics class: *Carpe diem, quam minimum credula postero.*

– 15 –

Stephen opened his eyes and turned his head on the pillow. The alarm clock showed 4:30. He slid out of bed.

After showering and dressing, he went downstairs to the hotel lobby and walked to the front desk. Again, there were no messages. He looked around the lobby. It was empty. Only the desk man, at whom Stephen nodded—no need for words. He walked over to the phone compartment, entered, took up the phone, and waited for the connection to go through.

"Hello!" shouted Elaine. She sounded angry.

"Sweetheart?" Stephen was startled, unnerved. "It's *me*."

"Oh good. It's you." An audible sigh of relief. She sounded tired. It was late at night.

"Ellie. Is everything okay?"

"Well, no, actually. I've been getting a lot of crank calls lately for some reason."

"Crank calls? Like what?"

"I don't know. Just someone keeps calling all the time. The same person, two or three times a day."

"You're kidding," said Stephen, anxiety building. Then going volcanic: "What the hell!"

"They never say anything. I keep saying hello? Hello? And then they hang up. *Really* pisses me off."

"It's not okay. It is *not* okay," said Stephen firmly.

But there wasn't much Stephen could do. He felt helpless. He *was* helpless. He fought to control his tone, to keep it even: "It's just a crank call," he offered. "Don't say anything. Just keep hanging up. They'll get tired eventually."

He said everything he could think of to reassure her. This was life today: telemarketers, crank callers, kooks were just part of Life in the Big City, life everywhere. Then he asked her about work, about Emily — small talk, although every detail of her life seemed portentous to Stephen at that moment as he looked out at the dark lobby through the glass door.

Then he heard a man's voice in the background, a few incoherent sentences, the words too faint to be distinguishable.

"Ellie," Stephen asked, his brows knitting, "is there someone else there?"

A hesitation. Then she spoke in a muted voice: "It's Ash."

"What? That guy?" Stephen was struck dumb. Ash — even the name infuriated him. He hated the name and he hated the man. But he was Em's father. He owed it to Em to remain civil. Jealousy — irrational, old as time, the dragon that slays love. He struggled to subdue his wrath.

A moment passed before his fury subsided enough so he could speak, then:

"What's he doing there?"

"He's just visiting Em. He's taking her for the day. It's a Valentine's Day thing."

"He's a creep, Elaine." Stephen felt the rage building again. "Stay away from him."

"I can't. He's her dad, Stephen."

"I don't trust him."

"Actually, he's being very sweet …" There was a pause. Was she looking over at her ex? Smiling at him? "He brought her a box of candy."

Zivko had entered the lobby and was walking briskly toward the phone booth. Stephen turned his back on the door and huddled over the phone.

"I'm happy for Em, but … I don't like it," he told her.

"It's *fine*, Stephen."

He took a deep breath and let it out. Let it go. He had to go to work. This wasn't the time for an argument.

"I just wanted to say I love you, Ellie."

"I love you too."

"I'll call you tonight."

"Okay."

Another pocket of silence …

"Sweetheart. The driver's here. Gotta go."

"Good luck on the film."

"Thanks. I love you," he said again, and moved to hang up. He yanked the phone back to his ear. "Wait! Wait!"

"What? I'm still here."

"Happy Valentine's Day," he said softly. He was still stinging from the image in his mind he couldn't shake: her ex standing close by, listening in on their conversation.

"I love you, Stephen, you know I do."

"Bye, sweetheart." His throat tightened. He slowly hung up. The click of the phone connecting with its cradle sounded like a gunshot in the silence of the booth. He closed his eyes tightly, and tears spilled from the corners—tears of rage. *Two crazy little peas in a crazy little pod.*

"Mr. Stephen!" said Zivko, voice muffled, rapping with his knuckles on the glass.

Stephen turned to face him. The young man was waving goofily. Stephen opened the door. He tried to smile. The driver grinned back at him like a three-year-old getting a treat.

Stephen remained standing in the compartment. Zivko looked around the room, leaned into Stephen and said, lowering his voice, "I got your VCR."

Stephen blinked, waited.

"In trunk of car," said Zivko, whispering in confidence. "Good price. Mitsubishi. Two hundred U.S."

"Great … thanks," said Stephen halfheartedly, still hot from the phone call.

"I took big risk, got you video you might want. You know *Beetle Jews*?"

Stephen confused, shook his head. Then: "You mean *Beetlejuice*?"

"Yeah, yeah. I not charge you," he said. He looked at

his watch. "Late again! But don't worry, Mr. Stephen. I got two *komplet lepinja* and two coffees. Turkish. Is very good. We eat on way."

Stephen nodded. More eggs, he thought, frowning. There would be many more to come—*kajgana, jaje na oko, rovito jaje, kuvano jaje*—all egg dishes.

He stepped out of the box—reluctantly, as he regarded the solid, mahogany phone booth as a kind of miniature home, as if his wife resided there. She was in there … with Emily and with her ex-husband. He hated every time he had to say goodbye to her. He hated it especially now.

The rational voice in his mind told him not to worry; she would stay true to him. But then again, had he stayed true to her? The rational voice told him to worry; she'd gone back to her ex before. The guy was tricky. They had a weird arrangement. The irrational, prehistoric voice told him, Get on the next plane and confront the bastard, and rid him from your life.

Love was indeed a kind of madness, he realized.

– 16 –

Lorenzo Barofio looked the part—"artist." With the viewfinder attached to a black cord strung around his neck, ever-dangling across his chest like a crucifix; with the big, brown, piercing eyes that examined you in terms of the shape of your face, front and back lighting, depth of field, shadow; with the dyed-black thinning hair and thick Tom Selleck mustache; with the Neapolitan olive-colored skin, the Humphrey Bogart cleft chin—Lorenzo was the quintessential Italian cinematographer. Although he'd worked mainly on low-budget action and horror films, some forty of them, he was a distinguished member of the Society of Italian Cinematographers and the European Federation of Cinematographers. He'd apprenticed under many famous artists, such respected men as Giuseppe Rotunno (*Amarcord*) and Pasualino De Santis (*Romeo and Juliet*). He worked cheaply, shot quickly, and his films looked gorgeous. The crew referred to him as Lorenzo il Magnifico. Stephen would rely on him like a patron saint.

Lorenzo listened intently to everything Stephen had

to say. He examined Stephen's sketches like a radiologist scrutinizing a set of x-rays for any signs of cancer. His brow was furrowed, his expression somber.

Stephen explained: "I want deep blacks, the frame filled with shadows, harsh contrasting light, tilted, expressionistic angles—a chiaroscuro look."

"Yes," responded Lorenzo, who was nodding knowingly. "You want-ta Caravaggio. You want-ta F. W. Murnau."

Stephen sat up a little straighter in the rigid plastic chair. He was impressed. Already they were thinking alike. Stephen knew, from his film classes at Cal, that the greatest directors had a kind of symbiotic relationship with their cinematographers—soul mate stuff. Orson Welles and Gregg Toland. Francis Ford Coppola and Vittorio Storaro.

"I want scary. *Haunting*," said Stephen.

"I geev-a you *hunting*," said Lorenzo. "Scary as *sheet*."

Stephen smiled, delighted.

Colon, who was watching everything, stood nearby. He looked impatient. He swiveled his head toward Borko, who was talking to the location scout, a young, rail-thin, harried-looking woman with a ponytail.

Colon pointed to his watch. Tapped it repeatedly. Borko nodded. Unspoken general's orders.

– 17 –

The park was not what Stephen had in mind. Not even close.

"Oh bloody hell," declared Colon with disgust, scanning the pastoral surroundings. There were drinking fountains, old men walking their dogs, little children playing football on the manicured grass. The trees were neatly coiffed. Green, bourgeois, under a pale sky. Buildings visible nearby.

"What happened?" Stephen asked the young Serbian location scout, feeling a surge of panic. She returned his gaze, a look of terror in her eyes.

Lorenzo scrutinized the park like a land surveyor. The cinematographer was thinking about how to salvage the mess. He would have to perform miracles with light and shadow. Special effects, perhaps, although there was no money for this. They could paint a cyclorama in the studio, possibly, a painted backdrop—create the illusion of a dark forest.

Borko, in his usual histrionic way, waved his arms in circles around him, like two airplane propellers, as he approached Stephen. "They screwed it all up!" he shouted, looking grave. "Lost in translation." He stopped the rotations and punctuated the point with a word spoken humbly: "Sorry." Then he shrugged his shoulders, as if helpless.

"I asked for death and decay. I get warm and fuzzy," said Stephen, half amused, half horrified, looking beseechingly at Borko. "You could have a kindergarten picnic here."

"I know. Never mind. I will fix it. I know what you want," said the production manager, sentences in nervous staccato.

Someone would have to pay for the time wasted. Colon acted swiftly. The location scout with the ponytail was dismissed on the spot.

– 18 –

They drove in a caravan of three cars across the *Pančevački most*, the E-70 bridge, to the northern bank of the Danube, where there was a swath of undeveloped land thick with deciduous trees, mostly black locust. It was February and cold; the trees had lost their leaves. Their twisted, gnarled branches and trunks were coal black; the sky, gray; the atmosphere, bleak. Stephen imagined Hansel and Gretel residing in these woods.

"It's perfect," Stephen declared, taking in his surroundings. He was elated. He felt re-energized. As he admired the grim terrain and the overcast sky, the clouds in his head were finally parting.

Flanked on one side by the set designer and on the other by Borko and Lorenzo—Colon had returned to the Avala production office to make calls—Stephen continued to trek through the forest until he came to a clearing.

"Is this enough space?" he asked the man standing next to him, an older gentleman named Nikola. He had the rounded shoulders, nearsighted squint, white hair, and pallor of a monk.

"Da li je to dovoljno prostora?" asked Borko, translating for Stephen. The old man listened carefully. He would be the man who would produce a haunted boarding school façade from thin air, like a wizard. The Italians nicknamed him *Nikola il Mago*—the Magician. He scoped the terrain, measuring and calculating with his eyes.

"Puno," he said finally. *"Savršen."*

Borko smiled at Stephen. "It's perfect, he said."

"Ask him how long."

"Koliko dugo?"

The old man thoughtfully rubbed his chin, white with stubble, then said, *"Dve nedelje."*

Borko: "In two weeks you will have your boarding school."

"Okay. Good. *Wonderful.*" Stephen allowed himself to feel optimistic, at least for now.

"After lunch, we meet in the office," said Borko. "You work on the script, planning for tomorrow … tomorrow you meet a few of the actors. They arrive at Belgrade Airport. Zivko will pick them up."

"Who, exactly?"

"Two of the leads, Ms. Ashenbach and Mr. Stiltz."

"And the headmaster?"

"Your Mr. Buckfellow arrives on a different flight. For him we have a limo."

Stephen flinched. *Your* Mr. Buckfellow. He'd had nothing to do with the hiring of this man, whose acting talents, at least in Stephen's view, were woefully limited. He'd hoped for an actor with better credits, more *talent,* a Terence Stamp, for instance—General Zod in *Superman!*—a great actor whose face had graced a hundred movies, someone who, if he'd been available, would have been perfect for the role.

Then Borko smiled enigmatically.

"What is it?" said Stephen.

"Tonight is big. *Big.* Are you ready?"

Stephen sighed, nodded.

"You have scheduled a dinner with ..."

Stephen's eyes narrowed. Borko's dramatizing of everything was growing wearisome.

"... the *ambassador.*"

Stephen's eyes widened. "Ambassador? What ambassador?"

"I am referring to the *American* ambassador. And his wife, of course. At the embassy, no less." Borko savored Stephen's look of skepticism—or was it anxiety?

"We have a production meeting tonight, don't we?" said Stephen hopefully. He had no desire to spend the evening discussing politics; he wanted to make movies.

Borko, dismissively: "You are, my friend, a film director from the greatest democracy in the free world." And then, with a verbal flourish: "You must remember that. You must do your patriotic duty." He placed his right hand over his heart. "As a representative of the great United States of America."

Stephen braced himself for the onslaught of the inevitable migraine.

– 19 –

C olon had prepared him for the evening on the drive to the United States Embassy, the only American representation in Yugoslavia. Stephen learned that Ambassador Harlan Hancock had been appointed to the job by Ronald Reagan in his last year as president.

"Reagan loathes Communism," stated Colon, visibly pleased. "He views Communist societies as bloody aberrations. Frankly, so do I. Good man, this president of yours."

As a Berkeley alum, Stephen knew well a small piece of Reagan's story. As governor of California in 1969 the former actor declared a state of emergency and sent 2,200 National Guard troops into Berkeley. Three thousand students had rioted and marched from Sproul Plaza up Telegraph Avenue. They converged on People's Park. Many of them had their heads beaten in with batons. Stephen attended Cal long after these events, but the notoriety of those times lives on. But he was a filmmaker. Nothing else mattered.

Stephen nodded to Colon, careful not to express his opinion. Don't talk politics when you're working on a movie set, someone once advised him. His film teacher at Laney? He couldn't remember who.

"Ambassador Hancock speaks Serbian fluently, as well as Russian and French," said Colon. "A little Polish too. When it comes to languages, he knows his onions — unlike you Americans, who are basically linguistic morons. So, it's best you keep your gob shut." He turned to Stephen to watch his reaction. Stephen remained unperturbed. *Gob? Working class.* "You Yanks," Colon said, using the word like an epithet, "*mangle* the mother language."

Stephen smiled, calmly resisting the temptation to protest. He was becoming inured to Colon's taunts. He looked out the window, searching for consolation.

"He's something of a folk hero locally, this man Hancock," Colon went on. "Tally this. Rather than travel about in a limousine, he prefers to drive himself in a leased Yugo. Ha! Ha!" he chuckled. "He'd leased it for one U.S. of A. dollar, bless his soul. They love him here. Absolutely love the man."

A military escort drove Stephen and Colon through the guard gate and onto the American Embassy grounds. Marines with M16 rifles slung over their shoulders stood outside the ambassador's house. One soldier opened the car door for them. They got out and approached the front door.

"Welcome," said the ambassador, who stood in the doorway waiting for them, smiling broadly as they mounted the brick steps. "Harlan Hancock." The gray in his hair at the temples and the warm, paternal, steady gaze gave him the look of a kindly professor. Stephen's mental movie reference was Donald Sutherland.

"How do you do, Mr. Ambassador," said Colon in his finest BBC accent. He'd fine-tuned the accent, Stephen noticed. "This is Mr. Stephen Krawczyk, from Los Angeles. The man I spoke to you about."

Stephen and the ambassador shook hands.

"Thank you, Colon, for once again for responding so obligingly to my request on such short notice," said the ambassador, now facing the producer.

"Always a pleasure, sir," smiled Colon.

Those damn yellow teeth again, thought Stephen.

"Please come in," said their host, as he gestured with both hands outstretched for them to enter.

As Stephen stepped into the entryway, he immediately spotted the suitcases: a half-dozen of them in the hall, packed and nearly blocking the door.

Seeing Stephen's puzzled look, the ambassador nodded. "Yes, yes. Sorry about the clutter. We're on our way to the airport, I'm afraid."

"Thank you for having us at a busy time," stated Colon, eyeing the suitcases worriedly. *This is unusual for Colon,* noted Stephen, *an expression of uneasiness.*

"No, of course. I always like to meet American filmmakers. It's always a special treat for my wife and me. We've always been big supporters of the arts."

"Are you coming back?" asked Stephen, feeling growing alarm yet prudently careful not to appear rude.

The man closed the door behind them and replied calmly:

"The country is transforming in unexpected ways. Slobodan Milošević is not the man we thought we understood. He is, shall we say, a new breed of Yugoslav politician. He has crudely exploited old myths of a Serbian golden age in order to further his own bid for federal power."

"You're jumping ship," said Stephen wryly, before he could catch himself. He looked over at Colon, who was now frowning, clearly displeased.

Hancock appeared unfazed. "He has already taken over the Republic's Communist Party," he explained. And then he added, leaning in closer to Stephen: "I fear it's going to get nasty."

A chill ran up Stephen's spine. He stared at his host, eyes wide with horror. He could not believe it. This could not be happening. Panic gripped him. He felt that his life was cascading more and more out of his control, a dread that something terrible was about to happen and that he could not stop it.

"Um, excuse me, Mr. Ambassador, but ... what exactly are you saying?" Stephen asked, exasperated. He threw another glance at Colon, who quickly looked away. Stephen stumbled on: "We've got at least three weeks of shooting left."

"Well, my friend," answered the ambassador, smiling at Stephen, ignoring Colon's glower. "My best advice is, well ... just be careful." And then he added—in what Stephen took as a diplomatic flourish—a wink and a nod.

Hancock guided Stephen and Colon into the living room. His wife was nowhere to be seen. *Hiding?* wondered

Stephen. He spotted a brightly colored oil painting. There were many paintings adorning the walls.

"Is that a Matisse?" Stephen asked, happy to find a distraction.

He walked over to the painting to inspect it more closely. It was a portrait of a woman in the Fauvist style—fiery reds, vibrant yellows, a diagonal swath of emerald blue. The woman was staring out of the painting, gazing directly at the viewer.

The ambassador and Colon joined him, and the three men studied the painting.

"Not quite," said their host. "But that's a reasonable assumption, what with the intense colors. No, it's a Nadežda Petrović self-portrait. She is considered by many to be Yugoslavia's most famous Impressionist. Do you like it?"

"I do," said Stephen. "I like the look on her face. Her expression is … what is it exactly? Is it deliberate ambiguity?" His feeling of panic had been temporarily tabled by the painting's beauty. "It's disdain, maybe. Or maybe it's contempt. Or is it disinterest? Or, maybe it's she can't believe what she sees. She sees *us*, and she's not impressed." It was a look with which he was familiar. He'd seen it on women's faces before.

"Right you are." Hancock was pleased. He was not expecting this response from a director of schlocky horror movies. "I see it as, shall we say, perspicacity?"

And then he tilted his head toward the painting. Stephen did not comprehend at first, so the ambassador repeated the gesture, nodded his head sideways toward the painting, and pointed with his index finger at the woman in the portrait's right eye. Stephen leaned in closer, carefully scrutinizing the picture …

And then he saw it. A round piece of something metallic that fit neatly within the bounds of Petrović's cornea. Stephen looked quizzically over at Hancock, who responded by placing his finger to his lips—silence. Stephen understood. It was a tiny microphone. The Yugoslavian police, the Communists, the Americans—who was it, exactly? *What am I doing here?* The embers of panic beginning to glow brighter.

The ambassador guided them into the dining room. A maid, a thick, heavily browed local Serbian woman, brought them beverages—a bottle of sparkling water, another one of wine. The wife soon joined them at the table. The ambassador made the introductions, and Stephen looked closely at her.

She was the picture of rectitude. Not a hair out of place, not an unwanted fold in the blouse—an exquisitely painted portrait herself. She too wore a cryptic expression on her face, like the Impressionistic woman in the painting.

The wife, Katherine, did most of the talking, about movies mostly, how she'd missed them here in Belgrade—American films in particular. The new Hollywood products were slow to arrive in Belgrade. *But you are leaving! You are running away!* Stephen wanted to scream at her. But he sat mute, distracted, a poor guest. He could not help himself; he was distraught. Then he looked up from his plate. He stared directly at Ambassador Hancock.

"If something goes wrong, sir, what can we Americans do?" He said this as casually and uncritically as possible, returning his gaze to his plate, dabbing absently with his fork at the green beans.

The ambassador only smiled. "If there is an emergency, Mr. Krawczyk—" Stephen looked up intently. "—and this is, you must understand, highly unlikely, we have a team remaining behind at the embassy. There are people here who can help you."

Stephen nodded, dubious. The ambassador gleaned the young director's unease.

"I've received ... *criticism* from some quarters," he went on. "You may have heard about the hunger strike?"

Stephen shook his head. "I haven't been following the news. I guess I should."

"No. You are making a movie, Mr. Krawczyk," he said cheerfully. "Why would you have time? This occurred just a few days ago. It was initiated by the workers of the Trepča Mines, part of a large industrial complex in Kosovo."

Stephen, staring blankly.

"No need to worry," he explained, shaking his head dismissively. "This is all very far away from Belgrade, in a distant province. A distant planet! The workers are protesting the abolition of the autonomy of Kosovo. It has nothing to do with us Americans. Nothing at all."

Stephen thought of the young people in the basement of the church. "And no demonstrations here in Belgrade?" he asked. "No repercussions?"—feeling indignation rising from within.

"There are indeed *repercussions,* as you diplomatically put it. Protests against the Slovenian, Albanian, and Croatian leaderships. Milošević loyalists have replaced the local politicians. Nationalism is rearing its ugly head, I'm afraid—" The ambassador caught himself; he was becoming too impassioned. He shot a quick look at his wife, who only looked down at her food, revealing nothing of her feelings, poker faced; but her admonition was clear in her noncommittal blankness. The ambassador, sighing deeply, returned his gaze to Stephen. The ingratiating smile also returned. "But you are safe. The Yugoslavian police will keep order"—said with confident finality. He cut off a piece of veal cutlet and lifted it to his mouth with his fork. "And with a new order comes a new ambassador." Veal hovering in space. "And that, my friend, is that." He plunged the meat into his mouth.

Stephen placed his fork on the tablecloth, sat up straight, and looked hard at his host. He kept his features impassive, his eyes unexpressive. "Okay, but, what happens if …" He considered his words. "… what should we do if civil war actually breaks out?"

The ambassador finished chewing his meat and swallowed. He took a sip from his glass of wine. "Gracious God! This is the best wine in Yugoslavia. A Podrum Aleksandrovic Regent Reserve Red, from the Oplenac region, mind you. The best there is! You should take a taste."

Stephen looked at his glass. He had not touched his wine. He waited patiently for his host's response, resisting the temptation to blurt out *What the hell!*

"What to do, you ask?" his host said, distracted momentarily by the taste of the wine that still lingered on his tongue. He smiled, in a state of bliss. And then, giving that wink-of-an-eye gesture of his, like a facial tic, as Stephen had witnessed before, he said:

"You get your ass to the airport."

– PART TWO –
PRINCIPAL PHOTOGRAPHY

– 20 –

It was the first day of shooting—Stephen's D-Day. Day of the Dream.

"Why are your nails so white?" Kurt Buckfellow said, scrutinizing Stephen's hands as they sat at opposite edges of a long couch in the Avala Green Room. Stephen already hated this man, and it was only the beginning of shooting.

Standing, Buckfellow loomed large, a brute of a man. He was six feet five but seemed even taller. At last he sat down, gazing menacingly at Stephen. Even sitting he was intimidating, thought Stephen. His face, square-jawed, hard as stone, was beat up from years of boxing, a hobby of his, and acting in low-end movies, for which he'd often done his own stunts, sometimes unsuccessfully, giving him a permanent mean expression.

"What? What are you talking about?" replied Stephen, confused, examining the back of his hands. The nails looked normal enough.

"They're *white*. Your *nails*. Weirdly so. Look at them! I've never seen nails like that."

Stephen was caught off guard. *What the hell?* "I—don't—know," he stammered ridiculously. He regained self-possession. "I have no idea. A hereditary thing, I guess. Maybe I need more zinc?" he ventured, smiling, regaining his composure. It was a strategy meant to throw Stephen off balance, he was aware, and it was working.

Buckfellow was good at intimidation and he was relentless:

"Your little movie ... Infernal *Ugliness—*"

"Cute," interjected Stephen, wincing.

"—will no doubt go straight to video." He marched on, undeterred by Stephen's burning gaze. "The script—if that is what you call it—is complete, unmerciful *crap.*"

Stephen held the stare of his adversary's ice-blue eyes. But Buckfellow continued jovially, undeterred:

"And that title! *Infernal Beauty*? An oxymoron, eh? A bit too esoteric for a lame horror flick like this thing, don't you think?"

"It's a thinking man's horror flick." Stephen smiled in momentary triumph.

"And what the fuck does it even mean? Do you really think those guys in Rome will go with your title? Not a chance. They'll slap on a tried-and-true title, call it *Horrifica Two.*"

"This film has nothing to do with *Horrifica*. Trueblood made that fifteen years ago. It's not even remotely the same story."

"Doesn't matter. It was a big hit. They'll try to capitalize on name recognition. That's how these guys operate."

"That's ridiculous," said Stephen, stifling a cough, clearly exasperated.

Buckfellow watched Stephen intently, enjoying his discomfort.

"Of course it's ridiculous. Your *movie* is ridiculous."

Stephen ignored the dangled bait. "Might as well call it *Star Wars Seven*, then. *That*'ll get audiences in the door."

"Nevertheless, despite the godawful script," Buckfellow went on, waving aside further debate with a swipe of his hand through the air, "I'm here. Besides the cash, playing a vampire tickles my fancy." He turned his gaze to the back of one hand, fingers spread, admiring his own flawless cuticles. "And by the way. I pondered your stage directions, Krawczyk, in your turgid little script. The scene where the good headmaster drinks Jennifer's blood." He cleared his throat and recited from memory, in a mocking Shakespearean, John Gielgud-like voice: *"He drinks her blood as if it were fine wine."* He looked back at Stephen accusatorily. *"You,* little man, unscrupulously stole that 'fine wine' business from the lips of Bela Lugosi."

Stephen, unperturbed: "So I did. Why have a cow over it? Hey, it's not like it's getting published, right? It's only a *stage direction.*"

Buckfellow shrugged his shoulders. "Doesn't matter. It's the principle of the thing, is it not? Anyway, your so-called *movie"* —he made a face and sniffed, suggesting he'd caught a whiff of something rotten, sulphuric—"is bound to offend everyone, on some level or another."

"What're you talking about?"

"I'm just saying, turning blood into wine, for instance. It's sacrilege!" he said, pointing a finger at Stephen. "A wonderful perversion of the Eucharist, you naughty man."

Stephen winced. "That's just great, Kurt, just great. But I wasn't even thinking about anything religious when I wrote it."

Buckfellow was undeterred: "There's more! There's also that business of the impalement with a wooden stake, my character's death scene. The way you describe it, you mock the crucifixion."

Stephen shook his head wearily and sighed. "Cool it, Kurt, will you?" said Stephen. "I'm not interested—"

"Neither am I, really. Frankly, Krawczyk, I just like sucking female blood, even when it's fake—and I love seeing you squirm."

Stephen sensed a migraine taking shape: clouds with flickers of lightning within. Buckfellow's face became blurry. Stephen immediately regretted what he said next:

"You know, I actually like your work, Kurt"—stated saccharine sweet. "*Stone Cold Dead* is a classic."

It was a bold countermove. Stephen was clearly mocking him. He knew Buckfellow would take this as an insult. *Stone Cold* was awful, and they both knew it. One *Variety* critic had written:

Mr. Buckfellow's erratic performance resembled a man in the last throes of a peanut allergy attack. In the end, his stone-cold acting left this regrettable film stone-cold dead on arrival.

It was one of many bad reviews in his long career. He'd hoped to forget all about it. But there was this tricky director.

Stephen, despite the superciliousnous of this particular actor, curtailed any feelings of antipathy as best he could; he understood how the movie business could take a toll on the more charitable side of the human spirit. In any case, he barely heard Buckfellow's insults; he was preoccupied with a sense of portent.

He'd seen the devastation before.

Stephen had received a phone call from Gaelen late one night in September, shortly after he and his wife had gone to bed. His friend had been drinking. He slurred his words as he spoke:

"Hey buddy. Howwww … ya doin'… man?" — drunken pauses between words, faux Southern California surfer accent. The voice irritated Stephen. Gaelen was always trying to act nonchalant, but he was wound tight like a cobra about to strike. But Stephen owed him. They'd met at Laney College, where Stephen learned basic editing and cinematography, and he'd been there for Stephen at some his lowest times. He'd also introduced Stephen to the woman who would become his literary agent, at least for a short period, before things got really bad.

"Gaelen. What's going on?" Stephen propped himself upright on the pillows and glanced at his wife, who was frowning. It was late and a work night.

"Dude, howwww … *come* ya … never *come* overrrr here

… any… *more*?" Gaelen asked accusatorially, words used as weapons, wounding Stephen.

"What? What do you mean?"

"Where the fuck've (hiccupping) you *been*, man?"

Gaelen lived alone. He depended on visits from Stephen, who was one of the few people who would put up with his friend's alcohol-fueled, vituperative accusations. It's precisely because he'd been an abusive alcoholic that Gaelen's wife had left him a long time ago. He still pined for her, Stephen suspected. She was frequently the subject of Gaelen's rants.

A retired stuntman, Gaelen specialized in car crashes. One memorable stunt was a six-minute piece in which pigeons fluttered out of the way in terror as Gaelen drove Bond's Aston Martin, which hurtled through Parisian streets at breathless speeds before ending up on the steps of the Sacré-Coeur Basilica. Gaelen sloughed off the dead skin of his life and his recurring loneliness by attempting lethal stunts like this, and by writing movie screenplays—his way of temporarily escaping reality. They were incomprehensible, stream-of-consciousness, testosterone-driven, shoot-'em-up action fantasies, and they always featured a tough, fearless, Alpha male hero. The scripts were routinely rejected by literary agents and production companies.

Gaelen always sent his first drafts to Stephen—another dreamer, a fellow passenger on the road to fame and fortune—script pages he'd written in a drunken state. And like Stephen, he hoped for affirmation of his life and, just maybe, forgiveness for his many sins. Stephen dutifully read the pages and wrote encouraging margin notes, hoping to alleviate some of his friend's pain. With each draft, he would tell Gaelen the writing was getting better, regardless of whether it actually was. To Gaelen's psyche, it was a degree of absolution. In a sense, Stephen acted as his confessor priest.

It'd been some time since Stephen had received any scripts from his friend.

"Gaelen, I saw you a couple of weeks ago. What are you talking about?" His voice rising: "I'm in bed!"

His friend's loud, angry, reproving voice suddenly dropped to a near-whimper: "It's been, like ... over a month," said Gaelen—stated flatly.

There was a long silence, and Stephen waited with dread.

"Oh. It's s'okay, Stephen," Gaelen said finally, leaning into the slur. "I'm jus' ... really sorry, man," Gaelen finally said, barely audible now. "I'm *really really* ... *REALLY* sorry." He used the adverb like a club.

Stephen thought he could hear sobbing on the other end. And then Gaelen, without another word, hung up.

Those were the last words Stephen heard from his friend: "really sorry." According to his ex-wife, Susan, who picked up the phone when Stephen checked in a week later, Stephen wasn't the only one he'd telephoned that night.

"He called everyone he could think of. Even me," she said. "Jesus. I hadn't talked to him in, like, a year."

Stephen was struck mute when she told him about the suicide. If he'd only thrown on his clothes, he realized, and raced over there, his friend might still be alive.

"Don't worry, Stephen," she went on, as if reading his mind. "There was nothing you could do, or anyone of us could do. You can't blame yourself. I certainly don't. That's just the sort of thing he would *want*—for us to all feel guilty," she added, her voice flattening into a monotone. "He was a cruel drunk. Pure and simple." Evidently, she was still angry with him.

There was a long silence. Stephen could not speak. Then he heard her voice again, softer now, halting and limping this time, as if just remembering her husband had killed himself. She told Stephen that she'd asked Gaelen why he was torturing himself, the movie business was killing him. She quoted him as saying, "I wanted to play in the big leagues."

Stephen always knew that Gaelen would leave this world sooner than later; the man risked his life crashing cars for a living, after all. So when his ex-wife told Stephen what had happened, he viewed the circumstances of his death not so much as tragedy, in the Aristotelian sense—there would be no feelings of pity and fear leading to catharsis—but as *irony* on a cosmic level. No. There were no tears. Not in the face of such earth-shaking irony. Stephen could only smile. Here his friend wanted recognition so badly he was willing to risk his life doing absurd stunts, no matter how breathtakingly dangerous the gig, all for some ephemeral *Big Dream*. But that night, alone in his garage, there was no audience. There were no witnesses, no affirmations of his talent coming from others, no person to appreciate this great sacrifice for Art. There were no cameras rolling.

Stephen looked over at his wife, who had gone back to sleep. Her face was turned away from him on the pillow, and he could hear the sound of her breathing, steady and deep.

It was for the best. He didn't want her to see the tears streaming down his cheeks.

− 21 −

They shot Buckfellow's scenes first. He'd agreed to take the lead in the movie only on the condition that he would swoop in and out of Belgrade, like a carrion bird of prey—or more precisely, a bat. The contract stipulated seven days. His flight was already booked, and Trueblood would not pay a lira more than agreed. There were other exploitation movies on Buckfellow's calendar, and he was anxious to flee. He was a busy man. Stephen would have to shoot quickly.

The first two days of shooting were taken up with expository material, all shot at Avala on simple sets. Classroom. Dorm room. Dining hall. Stephen decided to restrain himself stylistically, this early into the production. Master shots, over-the-shoulder, half-and-halfs, medium shots, close-ups—that's it. All camera lockdowns, no clever camera movement. The "money shots"—expensive shots meant to wow—would come later: oblique angles, crane and Steadicam shots, handheld shots; all the director's clever, visionary camerawork designed to highlight Stephen's style and cement his inevitable fame.

In the original draft the headmaster was called "Dr. Hamdon" and then rechristened "Dr. Caligari" by Stephen during the revision phase (his homage to the 1920 German horror film), played in an extravagant acting style by Buckfellow.

In the script's present incarnation, he greets the new students to the academy:

"We are so much more than a school," Caligari announced grandly. It was classic Buckfellow overacting. "We are a *community*. We are united in our happy pursuit of academic excellence ..." He reminded the young coeds to "do good as you do well"—dialogue bubbling over with platitudes improvised by Buckfellow, veering off script.

Stephen picked his battles. He let him alter the dialogue. His own scripted words were more buoyant, he believed, more inspirational—at least in Stephen's view. But Buckfellow dispatched the written dialogue to the artistic dustbin; he preferred to extemporize—and to snub Stephen. (He liked the name Caligari, however, although he never admitted it directly to Stephen. The name allowed him to create a character with an odd, hard-to-place foreign accent, something Bela Lugosi–like perhaps, but an odd inflection of his own devising.)

On the second and third days, they shot the vampire headmaster's seduction scenes—the "bite shots," as Stephen referred to them. Buckfellow was too old to play the part, however. The sunken cheeks, droopy neck, spotted skin like tea stains on coarse sackcloth—the debris of a face. The makeup artist could only do so much. The man needed a plastic surgeon.

The script called for a sexier lead. Terence Stamp had been high on Stephen's wish list, but Patrick Swayze would certainly have made the film a hit. Unfortunately, Buckfellow's take on the Caligari character came across as a letch, hardly sexy, and there was nothing Stephen could do about it. Half the audience's horror and nausea would arise from watching Buckfellow place his repulsive lips on the throats of his teenage victims.

Stephen set up the shot. He wanted Caligari to swoop in through an open dormitory window, backlit by a full moon, like a vampire bat—arms outstretched, large, open black sleeves of the nightshirt fluttering in the wind-machine breeze like wings. He'd had the crew fashion a harness for Buckfellow to wear about his torso, with piano wire attached. From directly below, the wires would be hidden by the actor's body. The wires were securely attached to hooks screwed into a Rube Goldberg contraption mounted parallel to the studio ceiling.

"You are out of your fucking mind," said Buckfellow, who fashioned himself a Method Actor, hell bent on *becoming* the vampire, not merely *playing* him, but refusing to do his own stunts. He said this with abundant indignation and glared at Stephen. He would savor Stephen's failure. He would be paid regardless if the film was completed.

"Trust me," was all that Stephen could say.

"Trust my ass," replied his star. "Use the stunt double, Krawczyk."

Stephen's migraine flared. Lights flashed before his eyes. He held it together by force of will.

"That's fine, *Kirk*," he said, discharging the name at him like a cannon ball. He deliberately used the actor's first name, as he knew the man preferred the more formal and respectful use of the surname. "I'll have Lorenzo il Magnifico keep the double's face in shadow. You don't have to do this shot. But keep in mind, *Kirk*," he continued, watching the actor coil like a snake, "people want to see your amazing *face*. The *audience* wants to see it. We want your menacing *good looks* on camera as you fly overhead. The audience should *see* it — your *hunger*, your *desire*, your predatory *love of the attack!*"

It was a blatant appeal to the actor's ego. It worked. Buckfellow's bloated self-image prevailed; he wanted to believe what he heard. He wavered, a crooked smile. *Clever man, this director.* Another close-up, another ego-fueling injection into his vainglorious veins. He acquiesced:

"An idiotic idea, but nevertheless. You are the director, I'm told" — spoken sarcastically.

Stephen saw red. Members of the crew, standing long the walls of the set watching, tittered covertly.

"*On je idiot,*" said one of the gaffers under his breath, although within hearing range, naively assuming the director would not understand even if he heard.

"*Lui non sa cosa sta facendo,*" said Buckfellow's stunt

double, Gio, shaking his head. He doesn't know what he's doing.

Stephen ignored them all. He moved on.

He studied his storyboard sketch depicting the headmaster flying overhead, the point of view from directly below, from the floor. He jettisoned Lorenzo's suggestion to mount the bulky Mitchell BNC on the set floor and angle it straight up. Instead, Stephen snatched up the Mitchell R35, smaller by half and lighter, and valiantly threw himself onto his back. He angled the camera straight up. It was a bold move. Many in the crew watched open mouthed, some of them snickering and nudging each other.

From the stage floor, flicking on the power switch, Stephen called "Action!" as he gazed through the camera's viewfinder. Two grips pulled hard at the ropes attached to the apparatus, which rolled—squeaking loudly, but this was a silent take—precariously on button wheels.

Buckfellow whooshed through the open window, arms outstretched, the black cloak fluttering gloriously in the machine-generated wind—just as planned. As he flew over Stephen, the director twisted on the floor, pivoting, the camera following the actor's arc through the air.

The director then called "Cut!" and he killed the camera's motor with a flick of a switch.

He was pleased. He got to his feet. There was a brief silence; the crew gaped. Then they broke into applause.

"Let's do it again," he commanded.

– 22 –

Trueblood visited the set on Day 4. He stood at the back of the sound stage, arms folded imperiously across his broad chest, and watched the proceedings covertly, unbeknownst to Stephen, under the cover of the set's peripheral darkness. Stephen was in the midst of rehearsing a shot.

The camera—the very same cumbersome 35mm Mitchell BNC camera used by the cinematographer Luciano Tovoli in horror maestro Dario Argento's *Suspiria,* shot with an aspect ratio of 2.39:1 to give the movie a widescreen, epic look—had been placed on a 10-foot track that ran from where Stephen stood to where his lead actress was crouching in fear. "Jennifer" was played by the movie's female star, Lizzy Ashenbach, a 24-year-old actress playing a high school coed. She was supposedly the evil "beauty" of the movie's title, although she wasn't Stephen's personal idea of beautiful. To his taste, she was simply "pretty, nothing special"; he had not done the casting. ("I need a nineteen-year-old Lauren Bacall, from *To Have and Have Not.* Can you get me someone like that?" he'd asked Borko at an early production meeting.)

In this scene, she was to scream to the high heavens, according to the script. No lines. Only a "blood-curdling scream," as the script put it. She has just seen her room-mate sprawled on the dorm room floor, the headmaster (Buckfellow at his lustiest) leaning over her and engorging himself on her blood.

"I can't do this," she said flatly, eyes narrow as slits, looking over at Stephen, who was standing behind the camera watching her closely, as if for reassurance.

Stephen must not waver in his self-assurance. *Benevolent despot. I must be decisive, directorial.* He took a deep breath and crossed over to the ingenue, who was frowning, forehead knitted, arms folded defiantly.

"What's wrong, Lizzy?" he said, striving to remain calm. He treated her as if she were a teenager in the midst of a tantrum—with patience. (Stephen chose to approach directing as an act of benign parenting. No scolding, no punishment; just "time out" in a corner, if need be.)

"I can't ... I can't *do this!*" she repeated, shaking her head, her eyes wild, baring her teeth like a feral beast. (She had the whitest, straightest teeth Stephen had ever seen, a look that would become the norm for actors in the film industry in the coming years—as ubiquitous as screenwrit-ers typing on their Macbooks in Starbucks all across greater Los Angeles today.)

Stephen pursed his lips but continued listening patiently.

"I wouldn't scream if I saw this ... this *horrible thing*

going on," she rasped. "It's *rape,* that's what it is! I'd be in shock. Revolted! I wouldn't scream like a child. I'd *fight!* My character just wouldn't *do* this. I mean, would *you*? *Really??* It feels like ... like *overacting.*" Then, with a final exhortation, like the last sneeze in a series: "It's not *real.*" She sat down on the bed, pouting, looking straight ahead, arms still folded.

Stephen did not know what to say. He'd had little experience working with actors.

Then he heard a whistle from behind. He turned to see a small, round figure of a man gesturing to him with a beckoning hand. Stephen had not seen this man in the studio before.

As Stephen approached, the man reached out to shake his hand and said, *"Mi dispiace molto. Mille scuse!* So sor-rr-rr-ry to inter-rr-rr-roopt your-rr wor—rk."—R's rolling thickly. His English was rough, but then again (according to Colon), he was a man who spoke a half dozen languages, *all* of them badly. "Max Tr-rrooeblood," he added. It was the boss. He reminded Stephen of Quasimodo, but with a pointy goatee (*real or from the makeup department?*), jet-black arching eyebrows (*dyed?*), incongruous with the gray beard. A rather homely face, all in all—big nose, pudgy cheeks. Charles Laughton in the 1939 film *The Hunchback of Notre Dame,* thought Stephen. The little man raised his eyebrows in a questioning gesture that was meant to convey humility: a what-can-you-teach-me look. All of it very disarming. All of it calculated.

"No one told me you were coming to Belgrade," said

Stephen. *Where the hell's Colon? Where's Borko? Why didn't they warn me?* They shook hands. "Nice to meet you, sir."

"No. *Nessuno sapeva.* I did not say a ting to no one."

"Well, glad you could come."

"No, no. Of course. *Il piacere è mio,*" he said, bowing at the waist slightly. "I like tat last shot you do," he went on to say, most charmingly. "Ver-rry good. Ver-rry inventive."

"Thanks," said Stephen. The visit was a complete surprise. Stephen had not prepared an appropriate response to a visit from his employer. He expected the higher-ups to remain in Rome for the duration, counting their profits on large mahogany desks.

"You we—eere loocky it wasn't a complete disaster," said the man amiably. If it was an admonition, Stephen missed it.

"Yeah, that's true. But we rehearsed it. Really well."

"Yes, but you should not waste pr-rrodooction money on cr-rrazy ideas like tat, no?" Eyebrows raised. He cocked his head in a way that reminded Stephen of a pet dog waiting expectantly for you to throw the ball.

"Right. I'll be careful."

Trueblood looked toward the set. "What is wr-rrong with tat actress? Why is she like tat?" he asked with a questioning look, head tilted to one side, although he knew the answer. Her mannerisms were all theater. He'd worked closely with actors for the past fifteen years, so he knew their behaviors pretty well.

"Well, actually, she's been like that since Day One," Stephen said. He took a deep breath but went ahead, feeling emboldened by the producer's seeming friendliness. "To tell you the truth, she's been a pain in the ass. She questions everything I ask her to do."

Trueblood smiled knowingly — all-wise, paternalistic, eager to teach this young beginner. He leaned closer to Stephen in confidence.

"I will tell you what to do. Fir-rrst, tell er-rr I said I wil-l poot er-rr lit-tle ass on de next plane out of Belgrado if she does not do as you say."

"Okay ..." said Stephen, wincing. "I'll be sure to tell her that."

"You do-a as I say," he said, eyebrows quickly contracting into a frown. But then the smile returned. "You ar-rre doing fine, Stephen. I ear — rr good tings about you. Go ahead. Do your-rr shot again. I like tat dolly move."

Stephen nodded, hesitated, then turned and walked to the set. He told Lizzy, voice low, that the executive producer of the movie was watching her, and he seemed unhappy with the way things were going. She should try to make the scream work. Forget realism! This is a movie that works *viscerally*, not intellectually, he explained. Lizzy looked into the shadows, squinting, biting her lower lip, and finally nodded.

The crew readied themselves, checking equipment, communicating with body language. They rehearsed the camera move one more time. When Lorenzo felt the lighting and the camera were ready, he nodded to Stephen. (They rarely spoke to each other once shooting began.)

The actress stood on her mark.

Stephen nodded to his assistant.

"*Tiho na setu, molim!* (Quiet on the set, please)," said the assistant director. "*Zvuk zvuka!* (Roll sound)."

"*Valjanje!* (Rolling)," responded the sound man.

"*Kamera,*" said the A.D.

"*Fino alla velocità!* (Speed)," responded the camera operator.

Stephen held his breath for two beats, then:

"Action!" His voice like the gunshot at the outset of a foot race.

The actress registered a look of horror as she looked camera right. She brought her palms to her cheeks, mouth open into the shape of a donut, eyes widening, doing her best to mimic Munch's *The Scream* …

She screamed.

Hearing his cacophonous cue, the grip pushed the camera quickly forward on its trolley and stopped abruptly once the camera lens bumped the actress's tortured face.

She jumped back in surprise. She fell back on the bed, utterly shocked. "It touched my face! The fucking camera touched my face!" She was horrified. She rubbed her cheek and looked at her fingers, checking for blood.

"Cut!!" yelled Stephen. He looked back at Trueblood, who smiled contentedly. Her performance was better than either of them had hoped for.

Then a general commotion on the set, as the crew repositioned the trolley at the head of the track and the gaffers made small adjustments in the lights. Organized chaos, thought Stephen as he watched admiringly.

The actress remained sitting on the bed as if made of stone, mortified, shell-shocked. Stephen ignored her.

Trueblood walked nonchalantly over to Stephen. He was clearly enjoying himself. He whispered into his director's ear:

"Ave er-rr do it again," he said softly, smiling innocently.

Stephen nodded. He set up the shot again. He spoke to his actress, calmed her down. When all was ready, himself still a bit shaken, he called:

"Action!"

The actress screamed dutifully. This time with angry conviction.

Stephen felt satisfied. He'd gotten his shot. He was about to call "Print it!" when Trueblood whispered into his ear.

"Ave er-rr do it again."

Stephen looked at him questioningly. Then nodded, obedient.

He reshot the scene. Each time, Trueblood asked Stephen to reshoot it—twelve times. Each time, Lizzy screamed until her voice finally went hoarse and her eyes brimmed with tears. After Take 12, Lizzy sat back on the bed, buried her face in her hands. Then she brought her hands away and stared at Stephen as if daring him to look away.

"You bastard," she said. She stood up and strode, her spine iron pole straight, off the set.

Stephen felt woozy. His mother's sweet voice suddenly entered his head:

"Stephen. Remember the Golden Rule."

He did not like this role he was playing, as director, authoritarian ruler, despot.

But Trueblood was enormously pleased. He spoke to Stephen, who was now quite frazzled: "You will-a no longer-rr ave tr-rrouble with tis one."

– 23 –

It was not until after they'd screened the dailies—always a few days lagging behind since the footage had to be processed in a lab in Rome—and had a brief production meeting at the studio that Stephen could finally return to the hotel. Zivko dropped him off at the Obrenović at 1:07 a.m. He'd worked nineteen hours that day. Tomorrow's call was at 7:00 a.m. It had been a week since he'd arrived in Belgrade, and lack of sleep had taken its toll. Circles under the eyes. Migraines becoming more frequent. Fuzzy thinking. Weight loss.

Before climbing the stairs leading to his room, he made a call to Elaine. She sounded tired, as always, but happy to hear from him. Everything was okay at work, she told him.

"Em made a new friend, named River!" she told him excitedly. Stephen was not sure if this was a boy or girl but decided not to press.

The crank calls had trickled down to once per day, which was manageable. All was going well enough at home. Mostly.

"Sometimes I wake up in the night thinking you're in bed with me," she said. "Then I remember." Her voice seemed summoned from afar. Stephen rubbed his eyes. He felt a rending inside. There was nothing he wanted more in the world than to make her happy, and he was failing.

"I'm so sorry," was all he could say, feeling psychically destitute.

"No. I'm all right. I'm managing."

There was another long pause as Stephen searched for the right words. She spoke first:

"Listen, sweetheart. You are the love of my life," she said. "Always remember that."

And she said this without any further clarification. An *a priori* fact stated, a kind of immutable Law of Physics or one of Plato's universal Truths. Like divine air breathed into him, thought Stephen. But as his wife spoke those unadorned words—simple but profound words of love— Stephen experienced something that can only be called spiritual. Holy.

After they ended their conversation and she hung up the phone, he imagined himself a marionette, and a Great Puppeteer in the sky was clipping the strings that held him upright.

– 24 –

He looked at the VCR, a big black metal box on the flimsy coffee table. A videocassette lay next to it: the hit *Beetlejuice*. Stephen was too agitated, too lost in a maelstrom of feelings, mostly homesickness, to watch a comedy—any movie, for that matter. When he finally laid his head down on the pillow, he could not fall asleep. He turned on the bedside light and lay on his back. He fixated on a crack in the plaster overhead. It rent the rectangular ceiling nearly in half with a jagged, zigzagging line. Stephen thought of a chicken egg cracking as an unborn chick struggled to break free. He thought of rips in the fabric of the universe. He thought of the crack in the windowpane in their apartment back in Santa Monica, which the landlord had refused to fix.

He tried not to think about anything. It was impossible. He thought about the night he split up with Elaine …

• • •

It was early in their relationship. Stephen sat at the little table in Elaine's kitchen. He was studying the *Psycho* screenplay for his film class, utterly absorbed. Joseph Stefano's writing style—clipped, economical descriptions of action, breezy dialogue—would enter his subconscious and later influence him as a screenwriter.

"I think maybe you should go," Elaine said, breaking the spell. Stephen looked up, blinking as if just waking.

Two wine glasses empty in the sink, bottoms still tinged red.

Stephen could not make sense of it afterward. He'd had too much wine, he acknowledged that much. He was also aware that he'd pretty much ignored Elaine that night, not really listening when she spoke to him, more interested in studying Stefano's script. *Psycho* begins with an illicit affair.

"What?" he said, momentarily disoriented. "What'd you say?"

"I said I think it might be better if you left now."

"What do you mean?"

She weighed her words carefully before speaking.

"Emily's dad is on his way over."

"Okay … so?" He listened gravely.

"So, I just thought you'd feel uncomfortable with his being here."

Stephen could not help himself. Reflexively territorial. Was it instinctual? Ancestral genes? Feelings emanating from some dark place? Nothing to be proud of, he knew.

"What do you mean, Elaine? Are you saying you don't want me here? If so, just say that." He pushed his chair back and stood. He closed the screenplay and tucked it into his leather briefcase, which he'd bought at the student store in Berkeley. A blue and gold University of California seal was emblazoned on one side of it. He zipped the briefcase closed. He was losing control, forces he hadn't witnessed before were taking control of him, alien forces, like in some bad science fiction movie.

"I'm not saying that. Of course I want you here, Stephen. I just thought you might—"

"I feel fine," he insisted, giving her a hard, uncompromising look.

"He'll be here any minute."

"You mean the guy who refuses to pay a dime of child support he owes you? The guy who makes sure he's paid under the table for every crappy job so he doesn't get his wages tapped—"

"Stephen! Em is in her room."

"I know what Charlie meant."

"Charlie?" she said, bewildered.

"He said you were crazy."

Elaine stood there: opened mouth, silent now. He'd made a mistake, but it'd slipped out. Too late. "You need to leave," she said with solemn finality.

That's when Elaine's husband—they had not yet formally divorced—arrived at the door. He was wearing an elaborate circus clown costume. His face was hidden under garish clown makeup. A big red nose. Long hair—long *blond* hair—was visible down the back. ("Longhairs" or "hippies" were an anachronism by the eighties.) It was clear to Stephen he'd spent some serious money on this ridiculous outfit, to please little Em—which baffled Stephen. Why the flagrant spending? Elaine had told Stephen that her "ex" was poor as Jesus. She'd said that he had been avoiding paying the $200 monthly child support, despite her frequent entreaties and a trip to a family law office, because he was always broke. He had not contributed one single dime to Emily's welfare in over a year.

Little Emily burst out of her room and made a beeline to her father.

"Daddy!" she yelped with joy. She had not seen him in three months; this was a special moment. He picked his daughter up in his arms and tossed her up into the air like a doll—a brief moment of panic in her expression—then caught her. She squealed with unrestrained delight.

"How's my little sweetheart doing?" he said, hugging her.

Oh Christ, thought Stephen. He felt his bowels rumble. He hated that term of endearment: *sweetheart*. She's only two years old, for chrissake, he thought. What's more, Elaine had addressed him that way many times. And he, her.

Elaine took a few steps back, as if making way for the Greatest Show on Earth to pass by in a procession, and clasped her hands together as if in prayer, smiling approvingly.

Despite his anger, despite his indignation, Stephen believed, and believed unwaveringly, even then and right up until the end, that love is the only thing that counts, that it neutralizes all that is painful and villainous in the world.

He would be all right; *Elaine* would be all right; *Emily* would be all right; *they* would be all right.

He gathered up his suitcase and his jacket and left the flat as unobtrusively as possible.

It was late. BART train service stopped running at midnight; he would take a bus home. After an hour of bus travel from the Haight, he arrived at the Transbay Terminal to find that the information windows were closed. The upper level was deserted. The next bus would not arrive until dawn. He sat on a wooden bench, its coldness seeping through his jeans. The fluorescent lights overhead cast a strangely diffused radiance, nearly as bright as daylight.

He splurged for a taxi. The nine dollars fare would cut deeply into his budget. He barely had enough in his checking account to last until the end of the week, when the university would dispense his next financial aid check.

After he arrived at the house on Blake Street, Stephen got out of the taxi. He thanked the driver and tipped him three dollars—and then, after a moment's thought, gave him another one to repair the psychic damage, to alleviate some of the guilt for his bad behavior that night.

As he walked toward the house, he stopped and looked back. He saw the driver still sitting behind the steering wheel filling out his waybill. Stephen blinked, and the wheel became a snake devouring its own tail. The cab's interior ceiling light formed a pool of light around the vehicle.

Once in his bedroom on the second floor, Stephen looked out the window. He saw the cab still parked at the curb, and he imagined that the driver was simply in no hurry to drive on in search of another lonely fare.

He waited for her call. He thought it best to let her reach out to him, as he'd behaved abominably and was ashamed. He believed, after what he'd said to Elaine, he had no right to intrude on her life, no right to speak to her let alone set foot in her little apartment again—unless she willed it. He did not hear from Elaine for two weeks. During that period, Stephen suffered from a loneliness he'd not experienced before—not to this degree, anyway. He figured, when you meet someone who could possibly be your soul mate—a term Stephen, ever the romantic, would always embrace wholeheartedly—all other relationships pale in comparison.

No, not pale; cease to exist.

– 25 –

He was busy, which helped—work was psychic balm. There was no room in his meticulously scheduled day for reflection or regret, for looking backward.

As director, he functioned as a psychologist, writer, visualist, parent, benevolent dictator. Actors and crew were drawn to him, pulled as if he were a magnet, by his openness, his magnanimity—they generally liked him. But that also meant they came with their unending concerns about dialogue or health issues; about lighting and camera placement; about the wardrobe for today's shoot; about the color of a prop. On-set problems mounted: "Jennifer" habitually showed up late to the set; Ron failed to memorize his lines; the sound man got sick; the set wasn't ready; the camera malfunctioned. Borko (now back on set and offering no explanation for his absence) savaged him with relentless news of glitches and setbacks in the day's shoot.

A week had passed. They'd shot Buckfellow's scenes in the classroom, dorm rooms, office. This would be the final scene with Buckfellow. The weary actor would be on a flight to the States that afternoon. There would be no reshoots.

As an act of revenge, as scripted, six of the headmaster's female victims have just nailed their tormentor to a dorm wall. The special effects crew had managed to secure Buckfellow to the wall with a clever harness hidden by his body; his feet hung two feet off the floor. Wooden nails, painted to look like metal, seemingly pierced his hands and feet—the effect was convincingly real. Arms were outstretched, deliberately mimicking—Buckfellow would say "mocking"—Christ's crucifixion. The scene worked. The violence and gore looked terribly real: the power of cinema as optical illusion.

Buckfellow looked down at Stephen from his place on the wall. The director was overseeing the work of the makeup artist, who stood on a ladder applying black shadows around his eyes with a brush. Buckfellow's face, a skull with cavernous sockets for eyes.

"You'll burn in hell for this shot, Krawczyk," he said flatly, voice like snake venom.

"Maybe so, Kirk. I'm more worried about a possible NC-Seventeen rating."

"Fuck ratings. Just make sure I'm paid and on that plane."

"A few setups and we're out of here."

Stephen stepped back and surveyed the final composition. They were almost ready to roll.

"Let's face it, Kirk, you've never looked better," he said, admiring the tableau. He was enjoying Buckfellow's helplessness. The man looked ravaged. "Who knows?"

Stephen added. "Maybe this'll get you a long-overdue Academy Award."

Buckfellow scowled. For a moment Stephen thought he might jump down from the wall and strangle him.

"Look, smartass," said Buckfellow. "It's a good scene. But we both know where you got the idea, this disgusting act of sacrilege."

"Right. *You* gave me the idea, Kurt, the script's religious implications and all that," he said. "But keep in mind. I think it was—was it Martin Scorsese?—who said, a good director gets his ideas from anywhere he can. If the craft services guy, production assistant, grip, focus puller, *anybody* has a brilliant idea, then use it."

"You're a thief."

"Okay, fine. Call me what you like—"

"Even stealing from real directors, like Scorsese."

"It's *my* name that ends up in the credits as director, Kirk. Not yours. I take full responsibility, success or failure. Guys like you go on to other films, regardless. But if this film bombs, I'll be forgotten."

Stephen regretted making the last point. He felt a sinking feeling in his gut.

"At the bottom of the billing. That's where your name will go, Krawczyk. As the star, my name will appear above yours." It was turning into a rant, his eyes brightening with fury. He shouted: "I'm the star of this picture, little man! Don't you forget that. All you need to do is make sure the key light is on me—and stay out of my sight!"

Stephen waited a few moments for the flare-up to pass.

And then: "Okay. You're the star. Nobody's denying that fact. So then. Act your pants off in this shot, Kurt. *Kill* it. Bellow loudly, like the pissed-off vampire you are—in terrible *indignation*." Stephen turned away and walked to his director of photography to discuss the positioning of the key light as Buckfellow hung from the wall, anger simmering.

The scene went better than Stephen could have hoped for. Buckfellow's bottled up fury—years of career frustrations, of producer abuse, of financial hardship—spilled out of him. Profane invectives, shrieks spewed out of his mouth like the green projectile vomit from Linda Blair's mouth in *The Exorcist*. As he screeched, the female students hammered nails into his extremities. Buckfellow—wailing, head twisting back and forth, spittle flying—acted up a storm. It was terrifying to watch. It was magnificent.

The *coup de grâce* came in the form of "Jennifer" wielding a six-foot long wooden pole sharpened to a point, then plunging the spike into the school headmaster's side. The allusion to the soldier's piercing of Christ with a lance was now made explicit.

The scene was ghastly. Stephen figured it could get axed by Trueblood—or, if released intact, might garner enough outrage to get the thing banned. He would take his chances.

Stephen shot the scene in twelve setups, mostly close-ups. Buckfellow's tormented face, the young women's befanged grimaces, hammers pounding, contorting torsos, blood spurting and splattering the dorm room walls—a blizzard of blood. He'd made a bona fide splatter film. Once the crew was back in Rome, Stephen would cut rapidly in the editing room, inspired by the seventy cuts in Hitchcock's *Psycho* shower scene. The impaling of Buckfellow would be "*I Soldi Sparati*," as Trueblood would have it: the Money Shot.

When he had what he wanted, Stephen thanked the crew, the actresses, everyone. The morning's work was solid. Before he left the set, he looked over at Buckfellow, who was wiping his sweat-and-blood painted face with a towel. They made eye contact. Stephen nodded to him, crossed over and shook his hand. Buckfellow smiled. And he was done.

– 26 –

He still hadn't been fired.

Trueblood was still in Belgrade, spending much of his time on set watching Stephen's every move while sitting in his special producer's chair—TRUEBLOOD was emblazoned in block red letters across the black canvas back—expressionless, sphinxlike. He always remained in the shadows, omnipresent, semivisible, watching everything. Stephen could not read him. Was the producer pleased with what Stephen had accomplished so far? The only feedback from Trueblood he'd received in the past week was a quick "I like-a what you did with de over-rrhead shot-a" and a simple salutation one morning—"*Molto bene, grazie*"—when Stephen had asked him how he was. *Watch out,* Stephen told himself. *Stay alert.* Nothing ruinous had happened so far. Stephen was still the director. He had not been replaced and it had been almost three weeks.

But he'd been paid the first twenty-five hundred dollars of his fee, a Starlight company check, which ameliorated his anxieties greatly. The per diem pay was generous and kept coming; he was hording the treasure in his suitcase. He would be able to pay off some of his debts when he arrived home. It was going relatively well. He realized—and this startled him, something as rare as a snow leopard in his life—that he was happy.

Stephen went to work. He set up the day's first shot. It was a dorm room scene in which Lizzy's character, Jennifer, now a vampire herself after having exchanged bodily fluids with the demonic headmaster, seduces fellow student "Chad." Chad was played by Ron Stiltz, the clever young man who sold frozen foods in Rome. Lizzy's face and naked body were coated in chalky-white makeup, applied meticulously to every square inch of flesh by the makeup artist Giovanni, breasts and shaved pubes included. Stephen wanted her to look like a corpse. A *sexy* corpse. A nude, ravenous, resurrected-from-the-dead female with bloody fangs. (It was this image of Lizzy that would grace the poster art for the 1990 release of the movie, which would be titled *Horrifica 2*.)

Lizzy dreaded having to play this scene. She feared that nude scenes could possibly ruin her nascent career. She complained vociferously when she arrived on set. She even confided in Stephen, in a panicked, brief huddle in a corner of the studio, that she was not feeling well and that she was about to get her period—but Stephen reminded her that she'd signed a contract. It might as well have been signed in blood, as far as Trueblood was concerned. The sex scene appeared in her copy of the script, right there on page 62, and she'd read it. What's more, she knew very well that softcore nudity was part and parcel to horror flicks, inevitable as the gore shots. She was not naïve. She was not dumb. (Stephen itched to say to her, "The show must go on!" —a phrase that originated in the nineteenth century during circus performances: If an animal got loose, the ringmaster would try to prevent the audience from panicking. Keep the clowns juggling, the acrobats swinging. But Stephen constrained the urge.)

Stephen had just walked Lorenzo through the blocking of the shot. When Lorenzo was satisfied with the lighting and the camera move, he nodded to Stephen. The A.D. prepared the crew, calling for quiet on the set. When everyone was ready—the moments before a shot always felt to Stephen like the world had stopped spinning, like the sun had stopped arcing across the sky as it had when Joshua led his army into Canaan—Stephen called "Action!"

The camera slowly tracked across the set as spectral-white Lizzy approached "Chad." He sat in a wooden chair waiting for her. Stephen directed Ron to play this scene as if he were simultaneously mesmerized by Lizzy's seductive advances and horrified by her demonic visage—a "deer caught in the headlights" was the script's stage direction. Conflicting emotions, perhaps, but nevertheless Ron strove valiantly to comply with his director's wishes. Stephen had Lorenzo shoot in low light and angled the spot so that its beam caught Lizzy's dimpled buttocks as she straddled her victim.

Ron took to his role with obvious relish. "Chad" took

"Jennifer" into his arms with a look of utter joy on his face. He was no actor, Ron—he owned a grocery store—but the look was genuine. As directed, Lizzy began grinding her hips on his lap. Nothing too graphic; no genitalia visible in the shot—"soft porn," as the industry referred to it. They began kissing hungrily. Stephen watched, pleased—the scene was playing out as he'd visualized it—as Lizzy grabbed Ron's head between her palms, flattened her lips on his, and plunged her tongue into his mouth. They kissed fiercely until Stephen shouted "Cut!" The two actors stopped kissing. More precisely, Lizzy pulled away, leaving Ron still pursing his lips idiotically, bug-eyed, looking like a gasping fish. They both looked about the set dazed, their faces flushed, visible through the makeup.

Stephen turned to the camera operator. "Did you get it?"

"*Capito,*" he said.

"Okay. Good. Print it. Move on," he told the A.D. "We'll get coverage next. Close-ups, over-the-shoulders. And hey: make sure the fangs are working."

"De bite-a shot, eh?" said Lorenzo who had been listening in, with an impish grin.

"Yeah, the bite shot, Lorenzo." And turning back to the A.D.: "And one other thing. We'll need the Karo syrup"—the fake blood that would spurt from Lizzy's mouth as she impaled her custom-made, retractable porcelain fangs into Chad's neck.

When it came time to shoot the scene, Stephen gave Lizzy direction:

"Before you bite into his neck, I want you to lick your lips. You are *thirsty*. And then, after clamping your teeth down and the blood spurts out, I want you to arch your head back—like you're in the middle of an orgasm—and slowly, *slowly* lick the blood off your lips. *Savor* it … like it's a fine wine."

She gave him a hard look.

"Hey, I know, Lizzy," he said. "But I want it sexy. The scene calls for it. And remember. It's only sugar syrup." He unfurled the banner of his smile, like a white flag on a battlefield, and then added as he turned to walk away, "With a little Red Dye Number Four."

The day's setups were on schedule. Two or three takes for each setup—a good day. Five pages of script already that day. (An average of two to six takes per setup; 346 setups in 28 days of shooting by the time he left Belgrade.) Stephen's shirt clung to his sweaty back.

As the crew went to work and Lizzy vanished into her dressing room, he caught an indeterminate figure in the shadows beyond the bank of lights. He stopped and stared. It was a woman he had not seen before. She was beautiful, in an exotic Eastern European way. She looked over at him demurely; he was the director, after all, technically her boss. Her red lipstick—it was the first thing that caught his attention. Then he took in the rest of her face. Nose bent a little. Features a bit asymmetrical. Blue eyes.

Hair so blonde, it was probably white. A tad overweight. *Unconventionally beautiful* was Stephen's quick assessment. He was transfixed anyway.

"Who is that woman?" Stephen asked his A.D., still gazing into the shadows.

"What woman?"

"There." He nodded toward her. The A.D. followed the line of his gaze.

"That … I think her name is – ček *'da razmislim* … Biljana! Her name is *Biljana*. She is set decorator."

Stephen swallowed, throat dry.

"Why haven't I seen her before?" —still looking at her.

"Why? She new. Just today. First time."

A familiar feeling came over Stephen. Loss of control. There was something inexorable about this encounter.

– 27 –

At dawn the following Monday morning, they drove to the forest location on the far side of the gray and muddy Danube—Zivko driving, Borko in the front passenger seat, and Stephen, Lorenzo il Magnifico, and Nikola the Magician production designer crammed together in the back seat. Stephen had to turn his body halfway to fit into the narrow space. Borko twisted around and handed a document to Stephen.

"What's this?" said Stephen.

"Visa. You will need this if we enter Romania. There is Meziad Cave, known for its numerous colonies of bats."

"What?" Stephen took the document, glanced at it and placed it into a jacket pocket, alongside his passport. Two Achilles' shields for protection.

"Temporarily allows you to shoot in foreign country. It is precaution. Many caves we can use outside Yugoslavia."

Stephen nodded. He hoped they wouldn't need it. He was even beginning to doubt the necessity of having a cave scene. But then, a real vampire cave instead of a tacky movie set …

"I haven't seen Colon in at least a week," said Stephen. Borko was now looking pensively out the window. They were crossing over the bridge, and the Danube—the Dunav to Serbo-Croatians—always held Borko spellbound, left him brooding. "Not that I've missed him," Stephen added.

"Yes, I know," said Borko, spell broken. He turned around and smiled at Stephen. He was deliberately being vague: *Yes, I know what you mean, neither have I missed him;* or *Yes, I understand that is how you feel.*

 "Where is he?" pressed Stephen.

"In Los Angeles, they tell me." Borko pronounced the City of Angels' name with a hard A—*Angle*-ess—and it irritated Stephen. "Two weeks. Maybe there forever!" He threw up his hands and spread them wide to emphasize the scope of time.

"What?" Stephen, now alert, looked hard at his unit manager, who he believed was his closest ally. "What's he doing in L.A.?"

"Putting deals together, *my* guess. Or making love to—how you say? To hot babes?"

Stephen cringed. "Wait, hold on," he said, feeling the faint beginnings of a migraine coming on. *Good riddance,* he thought. *No more sarcastic taunts.* But what was he up to? "I mean, aren't we supposed to have a line producer? Don't we *need* one?"

"Need Colon? Ha! He sets the machinery going, then disappears. He is like the clockmaker God of the Deists," said Borko, shifting into high philosophical mode. "Let me tell you. The Italians make movies like sausages in Belgrade Meat Center." He smiled as he contemplated his metaphor. He was hungry. "They can operate fine without him. What is he doing? Most likely he is selling *Infernal Beauty*—your masterpiece!—to a distributor. Maybe getting financing for another picture. I don't know! Could be anything."

Stephen frowned. It was a lie. Colon had bailed out after their meeting with the ambassador, fled Belgrade as fast as he could. Either Borko missed this or didn't care.

He was back gazing absentmindedly at the Danube. "Maybe he is hiring another director," offered Borko, shrugging his shoulders.

Stephen stared at him.

"Just kidding! Relax!" Borko chuckled, now looking at Stephen. "Little bit Yugoslavian humor." He offered an exaggerated grin. "As you Americans say: take a chill pill!"

But there was no relaxing for Stephen. And Borko's humor irritated him no end. He squirmed uncomfortably in the back seat, scrunched as he was against the door.

"No, no," said Borko. "He tells me nothing. I'm in, how you say, *in the darkness.* Just like you. So let me tell you. Those guys?—what is that American saying?—'march to the beat of a different band.'"

"Different drummer."

"Ah ha!"

"Thoreau."

"Yes, yes, of course. Your beloved Henry David Thoreau. I read this man at USC."

Stephen thought for a moment. He remembered *Walden* from Mrs. Welch's class in high school. He'd been a fan ever since. He recalled a line from it, which he'd memorized as part of a homework assignment, and which had become a kind of mantra repeated over the years. He recited it out loud:

"If you have built castles in the air, your work need not be lost; that is where they should be—" *You can achieve anything you set your mind to, Stephen ...*

"—now put the foundations under them," interjected Borko. "Hey. Look at that! I know Thoreau, like I said. We Serbs? We have our *own* great philosophers. And so I say to you, Stephen: '*Vrana ne odabira druge vrane.*'" He waited a beat, enjoying Stephen's puzzled look.

"Translate, please," urged Stephen, rolling his eyes.

"A crow does not pick out another crow's eyes."

Stephen looked at him questioningly.

"Watch out for Colon," Borko said tersely, his mood suddenly shifting, and he turned back around in his seat to watch the road ahead, cutting short further interrogation.

It was the second time Stephen had been warned about the line producer. And Borko was showing another unsettling side of himself.

– 28 –

There it was ... a thing of beauty. A marvel, really. Stephen could barely believe his eyes. He was pleased. A complete boarding school façade, built in two weeks. The construction crew had erected a convincing, and effectively creepy, Academy of Horror. Nikola—*a true wizard*, thought Stephen—had taken Stephen's sketches and added a few flourishes of his own. Behold! An architectural hodgepodge of medieval, Gothic, Tudor, Transylvanian, with a dose of unearthly imagination. The magician stood proudly alongside Stephen, looking over his creation.

"I love it," Stephen said. Stephen's mind erupted with ideas, Roman candles going off. So many great potential camera setups. Moreover, they could shoot with natural light: the gloomy, diffused early March weather was heaven sent.

He then conferred with Lorenzo as they walked around the set: detailed, handcrafted fronts held up by two-by-fours. An exquisitely beautiful façade; emptiness behind it. Stephen imagined the setups ... *camera goes here and over here ... Steadicam shot of the kids approaching the building, from here to there ... fog machine throughout the shot to give the scene a dreamy, ethereal feeling ...*

And then appeared the young woman's face. The bewitching eyes, the full red mouth—materializing, disembodied, in the mist. *Biljana.*

Stephen was staring into the ether when Borko put his hand lightly on his shoulder, startling him. "Oh, sorry. Nikola tells me you were asking about the new set decorator," said Borko.

Stephen was taken aback. "What are you talking about?"

"I'm just saying .... Look. I am your friend. You can trust me," said Borko, eyes pleading. "I know what you are thinking. That girl Biljana? She is a *lepa devojka*," he said, smiling benevolently, the wise older brother. Even the sound of her name sent ripples up and down Stephen's spine. "A very pretty girl."

"Okay ... and?"

"And what are you to her? *Listen,* my friend. You are an American movie director. You would be, for this girl, 'a feather in her cap'—that is how you say?—'A notch on her belt?' That is all that matters to her. She will go home to her girlfriends and tell her story, making them envy her." He punctuated the last remark with a quick affirming nod of his head.

Stephen said nothing. He did not know what to say, or how to take Borko. Was this man his very own guardian angel? Was there such a thing?

– 29 –

On Friday the drive from Belgrade to the Resava cave took two hours and twenty-three minutes via A1. They made two stops en route.

Zivko first swung by Avala. The production designer stepped out of the car and was soon replaced by one of his assistants, Biljana the set decorator, who would make notes and take Polaroids of the location. This decision, to include her in the creative team, made sense in that the Magician was needed at the studio that day; he had important work to do. There were still sets to be completed. However, someone from his team with a degree of experience had to see the cave and take photos. Since Stephen would shoot the script's penultimate scene on Monday—all the student vampires would turn to dust as the sunlight struck them—a special set would have to be constructed quickly, either at the caves or on an Avala stage. They could erect a cyclorama, a painted cave backdrop, on a stage, if need be.

The cave location was of relatively little consequence; the scene could be cut, if necessary; it did not especially further the story along and added minimal production value (in Colon's view, but as Stephen was keen to point out, he was out of the country). It was merely a scene envisioned (and prized) solely by Stephen. He liked the authenticity it brought to his mostly set-bound movie. Movies today, he believed, relied too heavily on optical illusions, *trompe de l'oeil*. ("The secret to film is that it's an illusion," George Lucas has stated. In the 80s, movies still utilized heavily mechanical special effects and actual location shoots. Lucas's *Star Wars: Return of the Jedi*, for example, featured puppets and actors wearing rubber costumes rather than CGI-generated creations. Much of the footage of Tatooine and the Great Pit of Carkoon was shot in Arizona. The slug-like alien Jabba the Hutt was designed by Phil Tippett and portrayed by a one-ton puppet, requiring three months and a half-million dollars to construct. Stephen did not have that kind of money at his disposal.)

Stephen figured that this maneuver—using an assistant rather than the Magician—could be viewed as simply pragmatic. Either that or something more sinister was at work.

Stephen opened the door and stepped out of the car. He held it open for Biljana, who scooted in next to Lorenzo. Stephen climbed in after her and closed the door. Again, he sat scrunched against the back door, but this time the person sitting next to him was a beautiful woman rather than the elderly Nikola the Magician.

They drove on. The ride was mostly quiet. Stephen tried to initiate a conversation with Biljana, but he quickly realized that her knowledge of English was rudimentary, not much better than his of Serbian. At first there were only small pauses between her words: "I … pleased … you … to meet." He asked questions in English: about her job at Avala; where she lived. The small pauses in her responses soon became vast oceans of emptiness: "I … you … um …" Stephen gave up trying to communicate with her. From then on, he decided, they would have to converse using pantomime, facial expressions, and Stone Age grunts. For the time being, they had nothing to say that was worth the exertion. They both stared at the road ahead in silence.

His eyes wandered, across the passing landscape, then to the woman joined to him at the hip. She was wearing a floaty, modern "ethno" outfit that was then gaining popularity in Yugoslavia. Traditional embroidery lined the sleeves. A long red wool skirt—a color that exactly matched her lipstick—concealed her legs. It was cold outside, so she cradled a wool sweater in her lap like a sleeping puppy. His eyes dropped reflexively to the cleavage above the border of her blouse. (It was a bad habit he'd struggled with all his adult life.) She caught him looking at her chest; his gaze lingered a fraction of a second too long. He gave an apologetic shrug and smiled foolishly. She smiled too. She did not seem to mind.

They continued to sit in silence, looking out the windows at the rich, fertile plains that gave way to limestone ranges visible to the east, ancient mountains to the southeast. Stephen glanced at Biljana only occasionally. Each time he did she met his gaze, forcing him to look away.

He became aware of her smell. Lilacs, was it? The name

of the flower just came to him. He was not even sure what lilacs looked like. *Lilacs*. Then he remembered. His mother kept them in their backyard when he was a kid growing up in Glendora. A waxy smell. Heady and sweet. It was a sense-memory moment from childhood but, while it was potent then, it was fleeting now.

It wasn't a flower at all, he decided, nothing of this earth. He thought harder. Rather, Biljana smelled like … heaven.

It wasn't just her smell. His sense of touch kicked in. Their two thighs, his and hers, were, due to circumstances, pressed firmly together. He felt her warmth through the fabric of her skirt and his jeans. He imagined wool and cotton fibers unraveling, one by one, into nonexistence.

The road took them to a small town.

Stephen sat upright, leaned forward, peered out the windshield. "What's going on?" A dozen men were marching in a circle, carrying placards bearing slogans, chanting, blocking the road.

Zivko stopped the car.

"Is Resavica," replied Borko gravely, eyes locked on the marchers. "A mining town. Brown coal they use for power plants. What you see here is they are protesting. It is very bad. A few days ago, Husamedin Azemi, Rahman Morina, Ali Shukriu resigned. And then ethnic Albanians refused to work. Just happened on Friday."

"We're not in Kosovo," reasoned Stephen.

"Yes, this is true. These men are in support of striking

miners everywhere. They protest ethnic discrimination."

"*Dolore nel culo*," muttered Lorenzo disgustedly, who had remained silent up to then. Pain in the ass.

"What, Lorenzo?" said Stephen, leaning forward, looking across Biljana.

Lorenzo shook his head dismissively. "*Barbari. Fanculo.*" Barbarians. Fuck it.

Borko twisted in his seat and looked back at Stephen, foursquare. He wasn't smiling.

"The place is coming apart. Bottom line. We must back up, take another route." He patted Zivko on the shoulder. "*Okreni se*," he instructed. Then, looking worriedly at Stephen: "You okay?"

"I don't know. I'm a little freaked out."

"Yes. You look a little funny, actually."

"I'm fine. Let's just get out of here."

"It is very complicated, you see," he said as Zivko backed the car, making a U-turn. "Milošević told a crowd—they were chanting '*Želimo oružje! Želimo oružje!* We want arms!' In Belgrade they would have revenge for *this*." Indicating the marchers in the road. "Now it is *guns* they want."

"Hold on, Borko. Let's think a second," said Stephen, settling back in the seat. "Maybe it's not such a great idea. I mean, shooting in a *cave*? In *this*? They want war, right? We're in the middle of some kind of *war*."

"Relax, Stephen!" said Borko. "It is in a galaxy far, far away. Like in *Star Wars* movie. We will be fine."

Stephen did not look reassured. The migraine threatened to return; he clenched his eyes shut.

Then he opened them. He watched as the marchers, one by one, began to take notice of their car. Stopped chanting and stared. Stared too long.

"Okay," continued Borko. "If it will make you feel better, I will arrange for a few soldiers to accompany us on the shoot. I can, how you say?—*make this happen*? I will call our friend, the American ambassador." At this, he laughed.

"Why is that funny?"

"Why? Because I just remembered. That man you met at the embassy? He is in the U.S.A. I totally forgot! He left two weeks ago. He flew out of Belgrade like a *bat* out of hell—the right imagery, do you think not?" He chuckled, enjoying his own wit.

"What the hell?!" Stephen closed his eyes again, twisted uncomfortably in the seat, Biljana shifting herself on the seat in sync.

"No, no, I was joking! There is another guy I can call."

Stay calm, Stephen told himself. By sheer power of will he fended off the migraine. *Maybe, as an American, I'll be safe,* he told himself. *This revolution has nothing to do with me.* There was a moment when paranoia was choking him. But then he reminded himself that Borko was a friend, someone he could trust. It was in Borko's interest, as well as Stephen's, and *everyone's,* to finish the movie.

They drove away.

– 30 –

They pulled up to a limestone hill and parked. As they got out of the car, Borko announced, "Resavska Pećina cave. We are here."

Lorenzo, Biljana, and Stephen followed Borko to the cave's entrance. Biljana carried a camera bag with her. Borko waved to the man in a nearby ticket booth, who in turn waved them through.

"Here we go, Stephen," said Borko, "your scary bat cave. Just as ordered. Oldest cave in Yugoslavia, you may wish to take note. Eighty million years, give or take a few thousand." He smiled and winked at Stephen. "If this doesn't work? We go to Romania—the most creepy caves this side of the Caucasus Mountains."

Inside they made their way along a spiral concrete path, passing through a hall of joined columns of yellowish stone. They entered a second hall and stopped. Electrical lighting illuminated the lower quarter of the chamber; the upper regions remained shrouded in darkness.

"This is what they call in English the Beehive Hall,"

said Borko, looking up. "As you can see, the roof is covered in *stalaktiti*. Stalactites, you say? If you squint your eyes and really really try to imagine, it looks like a beehive!" he said triumphantly, arms widespread, like Charlton Heston parting the Red Sea.

"How far does the tunnel go?" Stephen asked, looking for the exit, beginning to feel claustrophobic.

"Four and a half kilometers."

"Okay," said Stephen, feeling a bit dizzy. "I've seen enough." He then looked upward and shouted "Hey!"—his voice echoing off the calcified walls. They watched as the ceiling rippled surreally, like a black wave. Hundreds of bats alighted, an ocean of them, clusters breaking apart, flitting about feverishly overhead.

"*Sranje*," said Biljana—shit—taking hold of Stephen's arm and huddling against him.

"Flying r-rrrodents," said Lorenzo, giving a little shudder. "Oly Chr-rrist."

"This'll work, I think," said Stephen definitively, nodding as he watched the airborne ballet above. He had no desire to venture further into the labyrinth of tunnels; he hated the confining space. But it would look great on film. "It's creepy enough, Lorenzo," he said. But then, worried: "Can you bring in enough light?"

"We weeel-l need couple twelve-K M.I.s for sooch a big space."

"We have them?"

"I tink so. If not I wil-l get dem from R-rrrome."

Lorenzo walked off into the shadows, squinting, holding

his hands in a box shape mimicking a camera, muttering to himself in Italian. Borko wandered off in another direction, eyeing the formations, fascinated with the whimsical shapes.

Stephen watched as Biljana, pulling away from him — he'd put a comforting arm about her shoulders — placed her bag on the stone floor, unzipped it, and took out the Polaroid 600 camera. She aimed the sea-green boxy camera at a wall, flipped up the flash bar, and looked through the viewfinder. She pressed the red button, taking a picture. A photo slid slowly out of the camera, and Biljana quickly shielded it from the light with her hand as she placed it in her bag. She retrieved her pen and made notes on a pad. She repeated this process, taking several snapshots of the interior. Each time she waited patiently for the pictures to develop inside the camera bag; in a few minutes, they were ready.

Stephen watched her closely. She was wearing the sweater now. As she worked, there was a glint of white flesh where the sweater parted at the neck. His eyes kept going there — little helpless glances. Watching her move: aiming the camera in a new direction, snapping the picture and crouching down to deposit the snapshot, making notes, standing and turning. All this kept him mesmerized as he watched admiringly. She was occupied and yet she looked back at him after each click of the camera shutter, as if there was a cosmic connection, as if she desired a response from him. The snap of the shutter like the striking of a match; he, the kindling.

As she walked toward a popsicle-shaped stalagmite

rising from the floor, ready to snap another picture, Stephen moved to stay near her, like a moon of Jupiter, feeling her gravitational pull.

– 31 –

The drive back was uneventful. Stephen tried to imagine the camera setups for the cave shoot. Nothing was materializing in his mind's eye.

"You look distracted," said Borko, turned in his seat.

"What?" He was thinking about lilacs again.

"I asked you. What you think of the cave?"

"I'm not sure. Probably work." He was thinking about the claustrophobic space and smelling lilacs. And there was the impending war. "Maybe we should just, you know, maybe just send the second unit out with my sketches?" he asked rhetorically. Normally the second unit director of photography would capture landscapes, inserts, stunt scenes—shots without any key actors. There was no need for Stephen to return to the cave, technically speaking.

"Yes. Of course. You are right. But there are actors in the scene."

"Can we use doubles? The second-unit director? Shoot wide angle?"

Borko thought about it. "I'll send Miloje out here with his crew."

Stephen nodded. His gaze returned to the passing landscape.

Biljana drew him out of himself, asking: "Howwww? ..."—voice like a moaning cat. She'd given up on English. She redirected her question to Borko: "*Koliko još dana snimanja?*"

"She asked you, Stephen," he said. "When you will finish shooting."

"Tell her I don't know ..."—which was true. "We have the scenes at the school location," he went on. "And we have the final climactic scene with the vampires burning up ..."

"*On ne zna,*" Borko explained to her. He doesn't know.

Stephen didn't know.

– 32 –

That night, as he lay in bed staring at the ceiling, eyes wide open, Stephen thought about Biljana snapping cave photos. Her movements were sensual. He struggled to corral his thoughts.

He would think only about Elaine. Only her. Only her.

And then a wave of memories swept over Stephen …

The time Elaine suggested he stay the night after she'd broken up with Charlie. They'd shared a bottle of champagne. Feeling tipsy, Stephen believed it would not be wise to drive. He was beginning to slur his words.

Stephen slipped under the covers alongside Elaine. Elaine lay on the outside edge, Em next to her on the makeshift bed. Little Em, then two, was in the habit of sleeping alongside her mother in the bed, which was nothing much more than a narrow mattress draped with a lovely quilt on the floor, against one wall of her studio apartment. Em held her mother's hand and would not relinquish it, even when her mother reassured her all was well.

Stephen could not fall asleep: here was this wonderful woman lying next to him, her breath on his cheek while she was twisted under the covers, her leg atop his, a contortion act as she held Em's hand while simultaneously nuzzling Stephen's neck.

"I'm happy you stayed," she said.

"I am too."

"It's unsafe for you to drive."

"Yes, it is."

They lay quietly in silence. Then:

"It feels really good having you here," she said thoughtfully. "It's been kind of lonely."

"I know what you mean."

She thought a moment before speaking. Then: "I keep thinking about family," she said. "How small mine's become."

He asked carefully, "Is there anyone else in San Francisco?"

"Not anymore. My father died when I was little, and my mom died when I was pregnant with Em. Ovarian cancer. She never got to see her granddaughter." Her voice sounded brittle. Stephen remained silent. "I know it sounds weird, but I always thought that when she died, my mother's soul passed into Emily." She looked at him closely. "Do you think that's strange?"

"No, not at all. I think it's beautiful."

She smiled. How had she been so lucky?

"I have a brother—Teddy," she continued, "but I haven't seen much of him. He's sort of kept to himself after mom got sick. Last I heard he was in Ojai, somewhere down in Southern California. That was before Em was born."

He could hear Emily breathing steadily, now asleep.

"What about you?" she asked.

"It's just me. I'm an only child. I mean, I have two relatively normal parents, still married to each other, down south in Glendora, but we don't talk."

"That's so sad."

"No, it's fine. I grew up in a conventional home: middle class, a modest ranch-style house, two cars—the American Dream in a snapshot. You could use our house for an ad, next to a picture of the Statue of Liberty: '*Come to America and be like the Krawczyks, ye huddled masses yearning to breathe free*,'" in a faux announcer's voice. She chuckled. "They seem pretty content, though, from what I can tell. I guess you could say I went in the opposite direction."

"Are you never content?"

"Never!"

She smiled again.

"I guess you could say I'm the poster boy for the American Dream," he said with a small laugh.

"And now you're with this woman with a two-year-old. How the mighty have fallen!"

He shook his head. "Risen!"

She twisted her face to look at him with a questioning look.

"I wanted children," she said firmly. "Ever since I can

remember. *Always*. Problem was, my ex never did."

He flinched at the mentioning of her husband. He'd forgotten about this other being from another time and place. He hesitated, but decided to ask, carefully: "Why'd you guys break up? Was it the pregnancy?"

"We had an argument. Bitter. *Savage*, really. He wanted some friends of his to stay over. All of them idiots, high school buddies, none of them in relationships—*really* immature. But I wouldn't have it. I'd just had a baby, there were some problems, postpartum depression, they call it … I just needed my space. A little time to heal. But he insisted."

"Okay."

"We were in the kitchen. He opened a drawer and pulled out a knife."

Stephen froze. "God …"

"A little paring knife, nothing really. But it scared me. He waved it in my face and yelled—*threatened* me."

Stephen was silent.

"I bundled up Em—just a month old—and drove to a women's shelter in the Mission District."

After some time, still in shock, he said, "And you never went back."

"I cleaned out our bank account—most of it was my money anyway—and rented this apartment."

There was a long silence, a temporary gulf between them. Stephen feeling disturbed, rendered inarticulate by the horrible weight of this story. Then the rhythm of their breathing began to settle and synchronize.

"You're so lucky," she said.

"I am," he said, regaining his footing. "I'm here with you."

Her eyes glistened in the darkness.

"It's just me and Em," said Elaine. No regrets, stated as fact. Then she added, as if to complete the equation: "You … you're a good man, Stephen. I can tell."

The back of his neck tingled. Just then he knew that he was in love with this sensitive yet strong woman.

She turned her face away. He turned his body toward her, wrapped an arm around her protectively.

Then she managed to free her hand from Emily's tight grip. She snuggled up against him. Now face to face — her beautiful *film noir* face, those deep eyes. *God*, she was beautiful, he thought. He brushed a lock of hair from her face. She closed her eyes. She was smiling. Her breathing slowed. He kissed her temple and to his astonishment said softly to her, "I won't let anyone hurt you." And then, as if to cement the pledge, "I'll always be there for you if you need me — no matter what."

Their arms wrapped tightly around each other. She did not let go of him and he did not let go of her.

– 33 –

The following morning Zivko drove him straight to the forest location. When Stephen arrived, the crew was already at work, adding last-minute touches to the school's façade. Biljana, who'd arrived on the set two hours before Stephen and looked cheerful and spry as a fairy as she flitted from one corner of the structure to another, was pointing and making suggestions to her team:

"Dodajte još grunge tom zidu, više loze bršljana do ulaza, par balsa gargoiles i mnogo klizavih zmija tamo gore." Add more grunge to that wall, more ivy vines to the entryway, a couple of balsa gargoyles and lots of slithery serpents up there. (The snakes were Stephen's suggestion.)

The day was dank and drizzly. The actors were huddled together under a makeshift tent resembling a military bivouac. Halos of steam rose over their heads from their cups of coffee in the early morning cold, and they looked dour.

Stephen met with Lorenzo's camera crew, huddling like a football team before the next play. Lorenzo would shoot the entire scene using a Steadicam: a stabilizer for camera

175

mounts that allowed for smoother shots when filming on rough terrain. The device would certainly be useful in this gnarled forest, dispensing with the need for tracks or dollies, thus saving time and money while giving the scene a dreamy, trance-like feeling.

Stephen blocked the action, mapping the actors' marks on the pathway, Lorenzo watching closely. He led his actors—the leads and a few extras: students and locals with non-speaking roles—from a spot beginning deep in the forest and ending at the front door of the school set. He paired them up and then walked backward, gesticulating as he spoke to them. They followed obediently. He directed them to look frightened and wary as they trekked through the gloomy foliage.

Afterwards, once the actors had returned to the bivouac, Stephen discussed atmosphere with Lorenzo.

"We need mist. *Lots* of mist, vast clouds of it. I want the scene to look spooky."

"Yes, spooky," Lorenzo said.

"Dreamlike."

"Yes. I understand. You want-a fog machine. We have eet."

"Good. Get it fired up. Blanket the entire visual field with the stuff."

"Yes. Blanket … except one thing."

"What's that, Lorenzo?"

The usually jovial and deferential director of photography gave Stephen a pained look.

"The juice." He meant the mineral oil used in fog

machines. Propylene glycol is used rather than ethylene glycol (i.e., antifreeze), a close relative, as the latter is toxic. "Eees no good."

"Sorry, Lorenzo. We *need* the foggy atmosphere. We're making a horror movie."

"*Bene, bene.* I know. You geet-a your fog." He marched off, shaking his head.

Stephen spotted Borka drinking coffee and chatting with "Jennifer," whose makeup made her look like a garish Victoria's Secret runway model rather than an innocent 17-year-old high school student. He made his way over to the manager.

"Borko. I've got a question for you."

"Yes, Captain." He turned to face Stephen, who was cringing. "Jennifer" looked away, avoiding eye contact with her director, still nursing a grudge.

"I just gave Lorenzo instructions to ready the fog machine."

"Yes? This is good."

"He seemed, well … he seemed kind of reluctant."

Borko smiled, glanced over at "Jennifer," who was engrossed in a conversation with one of the extras, then back at Stephen.

"It is the chemicals. The mineral oil. You breathe in, gets in lungs, your body, *all* the orifices—it gives everyone the shits."

Stephen raised his eyebrows. "Oh. Great."

"The whole cast and crew will hate you."

Stephen sighed. "We need it, Borko," he implored, looking at the sky overhead. A bright day, blue sky just now breaking through—this would not do.

"I understand. You will have your fog!" He brought his hands up and waved them in the air. "You are the commander on the battlefield. What you say is law. Your soldiers will do as they are told. And as we say in Serbia: *Fook them.*"

"Okay," Stephen said, shaking his head, tired of Borko's histrionics.

They shot the scene: Steadicam operator walking sideways through the thick foliage, holding the camera mount with one hand, bracing himself on the shoulder of his assistant, watching the small screen on the apparatus; actors walking briskly, hitting all their marks, looking fearfully around them at the forest's dark spaces, then entering the school set, stopping to gawk; the yellowish fog enveloping them as if it were poison gas and this were a World War I movie.

He got his master shot and close-ups.

He got his creepy, vaporous atmosphere.

He drew out decent performances from the actors.

After the close-up of "Jennifer" looking entranced by the new school, Stephen called "Print!"—the last time he would ever again say that word on a movie set—and he made his way back to Zivko's Yugo, feeling a bit nauseous from the fog but elated by his success.

They'd finished in four hours, the quickest shoot to date.

– 34 –

Zivko brought the car to an abrupt stop. Dense crowds outside, on all sides: protesters were chanting, waving homemade signs, blocking traffic outside the Federal Parliament building in Belgrade's city center. The sound was thunderous:

"*Oamu ostavky!*" Resign!

"*Srbija je porasla!*" Serbia has risen!

Official Belgrade Radio would later say that about 1.2 million workers and students joined the rally in Belgrade that day, one of the largest demonstrations in the capital's history. The actual number was closer to 500,000. Big enough. The local government was in a panic.

Zivko sat immobilized, patting the steering wheel impatiently. Nervous anxiety, perhaps—he wasn't going anywhere, and the looming force of the large crowd felt menacing.

"What's this, Borko?" Stephen asked from the back seat. He stared in awe out the window. He hadn't seen mass demonstrations like this since the seventies.

"Jebote!" Zivko barked, slamming his open hand in frustration on the steering wheel. Would Trueblood reprimand him for returning late to the studio? He sighed deeply.

"Hundreds of Albanian miners," Borko explained, himself visibly edgy. "They ended occupation. Trepča lead and zinc mines. Cowardly provincial officials bowed to the strikers' demands and resigned."

Borko had good reason to fear the consequences of an upset to the status quo. His job as a production manager depended on a continuing, thriving film industry in Belgrade. But then, Stephen remembered the young revolutionaries in the church basement—they seemed to know Borko. His loyalties remained unclear.

Stephen watched in astonishment. "I don't understand. Why didn't you tell me all this before?"

"What? When was I supposed to do that? This morning? Ha! Ha! We have a movie to make, remember?" The good humor was feigned. Stephen could tell he was worried.

"I can't believe it. History in the making, as they say," pointed out Stephen, both alarmed and mesmerized by the protesters, their numbers, their chanting—power in numbers.

"Yes. You could say that," Borko replied, looking flabbergasted. The car remained stationary. They weren't going anywhere.

Whether it was a feeling of jubilation at completing the day's shoot or simply reckless curiosity—his being an American, a seventies protester in a foreign country in the midst of history in the making—Stephen grabbed the lever near his hip and pulled it, opening the door.

"What the *fook* are you doing, Stephen?" said his manager, looking over the back of the seat, horror stricken.

"We're stuck, right? We're done shooting, aren't we?" He stepped out. "It's okay, Borko. Don't sweat it. I'll be right back."

With that he stepped into the crowd.

Once engulfed in the crush of bodies, Zivko's Yugo now having vanished from sight, Stephen took in his surroundings. He'd never seen such a concentration of human beings in one place. Men and women, old and young, mostly youthful, in their twenties and thirties, some of them probably the young revolutionaries from the church's basement and the crowded cafés, men with beards, some wearing glasses, children riding on their dads' shoulders carrying placards.

He could hear the sound of a man's metallic, booming voice in the near distance, amplified by loudspeakers. He slowly worked his way through the bodies pressing around him on all sides. *The people, like a giant single-celled organism,* he thought to himself.

He moved slowly in the direction of the amplified voice. He saw at last a bald-headed man with tufts of white hair on the sides and wearing black, round, owl-like spectacles— Yugoslav President Raif Dizdarević—standing on a makeshift wooden platform, addressing the crowd. *Ben Kingsley could play this part,* thought Stephen—the politician's grin, lots of teeth, the eggshell head.

"Preduzeti sve neophodne mjere Jugoslavije kako bi se spriječilo raspad Jugoslavije," the president shouted into

the mic. We will take all necessary measures to prevent Yugoslavia from breaking apart.

The protesters interrupted his speech repeatedly:

"*Slo*bodan! *Slo*bodan!" Their fists likewise thrusting skywards, in unison, an amoeba, punctuating each repetition of the first syllable.

"*To je dužnost predsjedništva*—" Dizdarević struggled to declare. It is the duty of the presidency—

"*Slo*bodan! *Slo*bodan!" The crowd chanted, drowning out the metallic voice.

" *—da brani integritet federacije i ustavni sistem zemlje.*" — Dizdarević thrust his fist repeatedly into the air to mock the protesters: —to defend the integrity of the federation and the constitutional system of the country. The president looked like a benign university science professor under siege, a glint of fear detectable in the eyes.

The square was flooded with people, mostly young and eager for change. It was barely possible for Stephen to move one way or the other in this crowd. There was something exhilarating about social unrest, though, the pleas for change; Stephen watched in admiration. And then the mood shifted instantly. Stephen watched in horror as several protesters began throwing bottles. Then others tossed firecrackers and stones in the direction of the president's platform. Police started using tear gas in an attempt to drive them out of the square, but this only enraged them further, and they immediately began responding, some of them armed with sticks, traffic sign poles—anything not fixed to the ground. They jeered the police, chanting angrily at them to *"idi na Kosovo!"*

Stephen scanned for an opening in the convulsing crush of bodies pressing shoulder to shoulder on all sides. He then began to push and elbow his way out, to extricate himself from a cause he did not share, or even understand. It was their country, and he was an American, only visiting.

– 35 –

He found a small round sidewalk table at the Znak Pitanja Café on Kralja Petra, close to the city center, with the hubbub of the traffic and the chanting crowd in the distance. It was empty here. Everyone was in the square; most of the shops and cafés had closed. But this one had defiantly stayed open.

Then a woman sat down at the table next to his. She looked furtively over at him. Because he wore a congenial, sympathetic expression—a trustworthy face, charismatic— strangers often opened up to him. And Elaine had once told him he was the handsomest man she'd ever known.

She would be strikingly attractive if her flushed face wasn't wet with tears and lined with sorrow. He was reluctant to meet her gaze and perhaps become entangled. But at the same time, he was struck by the smoldering pathos in her demeanor, and it was difficult to look away.

He hesitated, then ventured, "Are you all right?"

"I'm sorry," she said, suddenly self-conscious, wiping away tears with the back of a hand, gathering herself. She looked at him straight, then down at her lap. She was taller than he was, he could tell, even though she was sitting down. Tall and curvy, maybe 40. Hair thick and unruly, framing an oval face with high cheekbones—a pale face, bony like a bird's—large, pale blue, watery eyes.

"It's okay," he said in an attempt to reassure her, but her expression remained downcast.

She introduced herself as "Minerva." Minerva wasn't her real name, Stephen assumed. Was it a *nom de guerre* she'd recently bestowed on herself? The Roman goddess of warfare, no less. In the short time that they talked, he learned that she'd had a fight with her husband at the airport, and he was nowhere to be found. They had been celebrating their tenth wedding anniversary by traveling around the world. Their home was in Toronto.

"I'm Québécoise," she explained, with a sweet, sensual French-Canadian accent that sent shivers through Stephen. "He's from New York. He was always correcting my English"—stated coolly, with a cheerless chuckle.

But when he, her husband, ogled a pretty woman at the airport in New York, that was the end. She'd had enough. They exchanged insults. He snapped. He struck her on the left side of her head with the back of his hand and soon afterward fled the terminal, zigzagging his way through the throng of travelers.

"He just …"—choking back a sob—"disappeared," she said, shaking her head in disbelief. "I mean, he was, like … *gone.*" She was fingering her paper napkin, rolling it into a tube, then unraveling it, over and over.

The epic scale of her dilemma was staggering. "He can't just leave you."

"Well, that's exactly what he did. I don't know. Maybe he went home." She added, with a shrug of her shoulders, "I don't care."

Stephen weighed the gravity of her response. She was obviously devastated. What her husband did was inexcusable, of course. Beyond wrong. How could a man do such a terrible thing to his wife? He felt a growing outrage, wanted to curse the man out loud, shout a profanity into the winds.

But he restrained himself. He breathed in deeply, then let the air out slowly. "Okay," he said after a minute of silence. "I get it. But Belgrade. Of all places!"

She shook her head. "I'm not sure what I was thinking. I just knew I had to get out. I booked the next flight going anywhere."

"Why not someplace like Paris? They have flights leaving every hour or so, don't they? I mean, the Louvre, the Eiffel Tower. All those charming sidewalk cafés ..." A more welcoming option, it would seem, for a woman alone on the run.

"Belgrade was at the top of the big board," she said simply. "The first city I saw. Besides, it's the last place my husband would go looking for me."

Stephen nodded. He tried to imagine what he'd do in her husband's place. Unfathomable.

"Anyway, I figured: go *anywhere* as long as it's not Toronto Pearson." She sat back on her seat, spine straight, and looked straight ahead, brooding.

He considered this woman and her story: terribly sad but at the same time romantic, if you weren't experiencing it yourself. Even after only a few minutes with her, Stephen felt enamored. It would often happen this way. Wherever he went, he felt dogged by romantic possibilities. Beautiful, interesting women were in every city, town, and village. If he were single, he might've offered his friendship to this woman in peril, might've explored the unknown terrain.

But he was no longer interested in any woman other than his wife in a romantic way. He loved Elaine unequivocally. He would forever remain true to her. If Elaine ever demanded proof of his love when he returned from Yugoslavia, he would tell her that he was ready to have that second child she'd wanted but he'd always refused her.

Their server, a young woman with dark hair tied back in a bun, a few strands falling into her face, brought them two Jelen beers.

They talked and drank the beaded chill of beer. Minerva was staying in a hotel close to the café, she told him as she took hold of his hand.

– 36 –

S he showed him her room at the Metropol Palace, in
walking distance from Nikola Tesla Museum. A 5-star
affair. *At least she has money, lots of it,* he thought as he entered
the suite. *Buys her freedom.* Modern décor: sharp lines, reflec-
tive surfaces. Black and red and white. Something Mondrian
might've dreamed up.

"Would you like a drink?" she asked immediately,
reaching for a crystal decanter on the bedside table.

He hesitated. She registered it.

"Anyway, I'm going to have a little something," she
said, pouring herself a half glass of amber-colored liquor.
Scotch? he wondered.

Then he said, "Okay," spoken half-heartedly. It was an
issue of chivalry to go along—a matter of dignity.

She opened a drawer below and drew out another glass,
poured two fingers' worth, and handed it to him. As he took
a sip, he thought about Borko, abandoned in the square
long ago, who by now had returned to the studio, probably

beside himself with anger. It was irresponsible, leaving the car. He should go. He'd have to take a cab.

He took another sip. It was Scotch indeed. He was surprised at how quickly it warmed him head to toe, scary how fast it worked on him. He'd had three beers at the café and now this. It got him into a mood of debasement; he would blame everything on the Scotch.

She felt he was watching her as she tilted her head back, closing her eyes, emptying the liquid into her waiting mouth. She put down the glass, sat on the white couch, removed her shoes—all accomplished with one smooth motion.

"I'm married," he suddenly blurted out.

She smiled. "So am I." Then she laughed and added, "You'd make good husband material."

He glanced at the door.

"Sit by me," she said, her smile odd, enigmatic. She patted the couch next to her—not a command, more like an offering. As if he were a puppy.

He stood his ground. She frowned. She reclined on the pillows, still watching him, keeping him collared with her eyes. A waiting odalisque? No, that wasn't right. Then he placed the look: Mrs. Robinson in *The Graduate*.

There was no sound in the room but the drift of distant traffic. He broke the silence: "I have to go," he said. He'd made a pact with himself. A phoenix rising. *Leave*, he told himself, *leave … LEAVE*.

Her expression had changed. Nothing wanton about this new look: vulnerable. He noticed the crow's feet for the first time, the exhaustion. Was it also a look of fear he detected? Of what? His instincts were to help this person in need. But he could not imagine how without sacrificing everything.

They both waited, motionless. A balance in the struggle between the two.

But then he sighed and added: "Look. We're both really lonely," fully aware that he sounded patronizing. He was fumbling for explanations. "Strangers here."

She just sat there and continued to stare.

He apologized, told her that he liked her, because it was true. He wanted to stay with her—two imperfect people seeking comfort, a long way from home. But he knew that was impossible. He would lose everything in the world he valued. He would lose Elaine.

She closed her eyes, weariness descending upon her, and slowly twisted her head back and forth, cracking some bones in her neck.

She opened her eyes. She stood decisively.

"It would be a mistake," he said simply. The torn fabric of the universe must be mended.

She turned away from him—it was a gamble. "Then let's make a mistake together," she said as she slowly walked toward the bedroom. Very slowly, tentatively, she looked over her shoulder.

Was he a Good Samaritan? A chivalrous knight? A father figure? A stand-in for the husband she'd lost? He was an idiot.

– 37 –

He grabbed a *gibanica* egg and cheese pie on the way — it would have to fortify him for the shoot and maybe into the night.

I am the Egg Man, thought Stephen. *A fool on the hill.*

"Minerva. Goddess of War," Stephen muttered.

"*Šta si rekao*?" asked the driver puzzled, looking over his shoulder at his funny passenger. Another crazy foreigner.

"Nothing," replied Stephen.

Stephen jogged down the long studio hallway, a colorless tunnel void of any wall decorations. Usually there are framed stills of movies on every wall of studios. Avala was more an abandoned factory building than a typical studio. Nothing the least romantic about the place.

When Stephen finally arrived at the sound stage, Borko only stared at him silently, a sullen expression.

"We ready?" Stephen asked, a half-smile signaling regret.

"A lot of excitement today, Captain Ahab?" said Borko, grinning absurdly.

Stephen winced, said nothing. His head ached. He hadn't had time to brush his teeth. Did he still smell of Scotch?

"We thought maybe you got lost in the square."

"I think I did."

Borko nodded, turned and walked away from him, walked toward the set. "We're behind schedule," he said.

Biljana was making last-minute adjustments to the set—a classroom. She approached Stephen, who was watching her intently.

"Eees hokay?" she asked, indicating the whiteboard on the wall behind the desk. Teacher's notes in chalk:

> Because I could not stop for Death—
> He kindly stopped for me—
> The Carriage held but just Ourselves—
> And Immortality.
> —Emily Dickinson

It was a last-minute flash of inspiration on Stephen's part. It wasn't in the script. But it was an English class, and something should be on the board, he reasoned.

"Yes. Perfect. Thank you, Biljana," he replied. She smiled, eyes meeting his briefly, then rubbed her hands together, shook off the chalk dust, and walked off the set.

The plan was that in this shot the students, twenty of them, would be sitting in their seats in neat rows. Six were actual actors, the others, extras. The teacher, played by a beloved local Serbian actress, fiftyish, dyed red hair, attractive, stood facing her students.

Stephen had asked the D.P. to place a track down the length of one of the aisles between the desks. The Mitchell was mounted on a dolly and the camera crew stood at the ready.

The makeup and special effects team had done their work. They watched expectantly from the sidelines.

The camera angled in a locked-down shot of the actress speaking to the class: "Shall we start with you, Jennifer?" The "teacher" indicated the poem on the board as she asked: "What would you say this poem is about?"

"Cut!" Stephen called out. "Print"—one take and move on, he directed.

The assistant director looked surprised. "You wish one more take? To be safe?"

"No." Stephen was impatient, aware of his lateness, the endangered schedule.

After 45 minutes of general commotion on the set, the camera angle had been reversed. Stephen rehearsed the actors, the camera crew's moves. When he felt they were ready, he nodded to the assistant director.

"*Tiho na setu, molim!*" said the A.D. "*Zvuk zvuka!*"

"*Valjanje!*" responded the sound man.

"*Kamera,*" said the A.D.

"*Fino alla velocità!*" responded the camera operator.

A camera assistant—holding the clapboard open, displaying scene and take—clapped it closed, thus synchronizing of picture and sound.

Stephen held his breath for two beats, then said softly, the only sound on the hushed stage:

"Action."

The scene played out. The grip pushed the dolly slowly. The student to the right, young Ron, leaned forward, panicked. The camera caught the drop of blood falling from his nose. He looked with shock at the blood splotch on his notes.

Then the camera moved forward without slowing, settling on the next student in the row, a young woman we have not seen before, hair in pigtails to make her look younger, coming into the shot; she coughed, and blood sprayed on her open notebook. A look of horror on her face.

The camera smoothly progresses to the next student, who fills the frame and stops. It is "Jennifer" looking fierce, eyes blazing bright as she stares ahead. Then she screams like a banshee. Fangs sprouting from her gums and blood flowing from the corners of her eyes, she shouts at the teacher, "I—don't—know!!" Her answer to the question asked an hour earlier.

"Cut!" shouted Stephen.

He stepped forward, stopped, flanked "Jennifer."

"You okay?" he asked her.

The burning look in her eyes said it all: Don't ask.

– 38 –

It was midnight. After sorting out the details for the next day's shoot in their daily production meeting, the crew journeyed through the labyrinthine maze of Avala's corridors to the screening room.

Stephen sat alone near the back of the small theater; the camera team sat in a clump midway down the sloping plane of seats; others, dark spectral shapes, were scattered about the theater. Trueblood as always sat on an aisle seat next to Borko, eight rows down, his back to Stephen, who was miserable. It'd been a long day.

He hated these sessions. His work would be scrutinized carefully, criticism would assail him without pity. He braced himself …

The workprint filled the screen. The images were rough, unedited, with the clapperboard heading each take. *Il Vampiro/Director: Krawczyk/Roll 38/Scene 75C/Take 1*. Stephen gritted his teeth, face turning crimson in embarrassment as he watched "Jennifer" standing under steamy, cascading water (real steam; the water was scalding hot) in the dorm's shower room. Trueblood insisted on this gratuitous nudity, as he knew it would help increase market sales. This was not a matter of "artistically justifiable nudity"—there was no attempt made at creating art. It was unadulterated greed. Trueblood understood that his audience expected to see "full-frontal" nudity and graphic violence; they came with the genre and would sell tickets. Stephen understood the rules. So did the actress playing Jennifer. However, when it came time to shoot the shower scene, she complained riotously. Stephen had to calm her down using his diplomacy. He reminded her again of her contract, though, which included a nudity clause; she'd signed it.

"Look. I'll shoot it as tastefully as I can," Stephen had told her sincerely, although "taste" was as subjective as "beauty." "Anyway, listen. You have a beautiful body. That's just a fact. You can be proud of how you look." And as an afterthought: "Hey. It's only twenty seconds of screen time."

She only glared at him silently. She wasn't buying it. Still, she knew it was either shoot this scene or catch the next flight out of Belgrade, forfeiting the remaining $2,500 Trueblood owed her and risking having her scenes cut from the finished product. Starlight would find a replacement and reshoot her scenes with a more compliant actress.

Stephen rubbed his eyes with his fingers, looking down, as the scene played out on the screen—he couldn't watch. He actually hated this stuff, felt he was somehow breaking some code, but he'd already broken so many codes. He'd begun the shot with a closeup of "Jennifer's" feet and calves, hot water splashing down on the tile floor (the steam was real), blood running down her legs and spiraling down a drain (Stephen's homage to Hitchcock). Then the camera rose slowly upwards on the dolly's hydraulic lift, gradually revealing her thighs, then the genitalia, the abdomen, breasts, and finally settling on her face. She had her head thrown back, mouth open in feigned ecstasy, exposing her bloody vampire fangs, the powerful stream of water from the shower head striking her face and exploding in a Roman candle burst of reddish spray.

Stephen had shot four more takes—not because he enjoyed watching her writhe naked under the deluge but because the camera lift kept snagging on its upward movement and ruining the shot—and he squirmed uncomfortably in his chair as each take unfurled on the screen.

When the lights came up, Trueblood turned in his chair and looked for Stephen. Spotting him at last, he screamed:

"What was that?" he shouted, in clear English. He spoke loud enough to be heard even outside the screening room. Then he fell back on the accent: "Why-a so queeek?"

"What do you mean?" said Stephen.

"The shot! It eees too fast."

Stephen sighed. Then: "We can shoot it again."

"No. *Non sta succedendo.* We move on!" Then turning to Borko and muttering, *"Fottuto idiota."*

As Zivko drove him back into the city, it was just after midnight. The day's call was set for eight a.m. He wondered why Trueblood bothered with a hotel for the crew; they should set up beds at Avala.

But he was too wound up from the day. And he wondered what Minerva was doing.

By the time he finally made it back to the hotel, he was exhausted. More than exhausted. His body was running down and was showing signs of deterioration: the gaunt look, the hunched posture, the frequent headaches. He fell onto the bed without taking off his clothes and was out.

But sometime in the middle of the night he woke up and lay there, eyes open in the darkness, deathly absolute. He thought about Minerva, but then about Elaine. He was not growing accustomed to the loneliness, as he'd hoped he would. It was getting worse.

– 39 –

The next morning he asked Zivko to stop by the Metropol before heading back to the studio.

When he faced the concierge at the front desk to inquire about Minerva—he'd decided to leave her a note—he was told they had nobody staying there named "Minerva." Of course, thought Stephen; it wasn't her real name.

"She's the woman staying in room Twenty-Two-Oh-Two."

"Ah, yessir," the smiling, well-groomed, mustachioed man replied. "Mrs. McLeod." Stephen was surprised. Somehow her personality didn't fit the name. She was Minerva. The fearless warrior goddess. "She check out this morning."

Stephen just stared.

"Sir?" asked the concierge, waiting.

Stephen recovered. "Did she leave a note?"

"A note?

"A message. Um … a *poruka*."

"Let me see." The man checked beneath the counter, then the box for room 2202. "No, sir. No is *poruka*."

The two men looked at each other, in a stalemate.

"Anything else I can help you with, sir?"

"Nothing," said Stephen. He turned toward the exit. "Nothing"—barely audible, more to himself. He was engulfed in a brief fit of remorse, of incomprehension, anger, sadness, the whole gamut of feelings, visible to no one.

Then he headed straight out into the gray morning without a glance back.

– PART THREE –
POST-PRODUCTION

– 40 –

They'd nearly finished location shooting.

Back at the hotel, as he crossed the lobby on his way to the stairs, Stephen noticed two men on a small couch, sitting uncomfortably close together; they leaned away from each other at their waists, their figures forming a V. Both men were impeccably dressed—conspicuously so—in similar well-cut blue suits but with ties of starkly different colors: one a royal blue with white stripes, the other a nauseous shade of green. The one with the blue tie was a handsome man, Stephen saw, but—now he was just feet away as he approached them—he noticed bags under the eyes and a weariness that reminded Stephen of a man who had been waiting at a bus stop too long. He looked bored. With his harshly combed-back grey hair, receding dramatically at the temples, and his large, bulbous head, Blue Tie reminded Stephen of Orson Welles in *Citizen Kane.*

This was Citizen Milošević. For a moment or two Stephen stood staring. He recognized the man from news-papers he'd seen at corner newsstands all over Belgrade.

He did not know it yet, but that very morning, Milošević had presided over a session of the Serbian parliament that voted to reabsorb both Kosovo and Vojvodina into Serbia. Milošević had declared a state of emergency: direct rule from Belgrade over those provinces. His star rapidly on the rise, he'd already achieved celebrity status in the Serbian capital. Stephen understood stardom: doors opened for stars in Hollywood and everywhere else. He seized the opportunity. He introduced himself.

"Mr. Milošević," said Stephen, as if he were addressing someone on the red carpet, although he knew next to nothing about this politician other than what the headlines shouted. "I'm Stephen Crawford. An American—um, visiting," he added awkwardly.

Milošević turned his eyes on Stephen. "American?" The man began to brighten, eyes suddenly focusing more closely on the stranger. The other man, Green Tie, likely a devoted underling of some kind, was still leaning to the side. He angled his head to gain a better look at this brazen American, presenting a quizzical, comic, Buster Keatonish image.

"We're making a movie here." Stephen smiled inanely, suddenly feeling awkward; making movies in the real world. "*Infernal Beauty*," he added with pride.

As if to offer an explanation for his presence in the hotel, certainly not the best in Belgrade, Milošević tilted his head in the direction of the restaurant. "Is very good *Karađorđeva šnicla* here. Have you tried it?"

Stephen shook his head, shrugged his shoulders. He

hadn't had time to visit the hotel restaurant. He felt as if he hadn't had time to sleep.

Green tie, a growing worried look, suddenly interjected: "Slobo—"

Milošević shot back a reprimanding glower and returned Stephen's smile with an even broader one while extending his hand. Stephen shook it, although the man remained seated. The boyish grin and lower physical position in relation to Stephen gave him a mildly deferential demeanor.

Stephen said, "I've read about you in the papers."

Milošević said, "Yes. The Kosovo problem." He spoke English with only the faintest of accents, Stephen noted: obviously an educated man, worldly, a lawyer. "I admire your Hollywood. Especially your Disney cartoons." He was now smiling broadly, eyes closed, face crinkled in pleasure, perhaps recalling a scene from *Cinderella.*

Stephen looked at this man who was grinning with such fresh-faced delight. *Banality triumphant,* he thought.

But the smile quickly faded. "I tell you secret," Milošević began, leaning slightly towards Stephen as his voice lowered to a conspiratorial tone. "What we are doing." His face now dark. Stephen tensed. Had Stephen been too bold, too bumptious? Had he said something wrong? "I really don't believe if you show it to any honest American—yourself for instance—that this one single honest American will tell you that if we were on a place of our delegation who sign, we are talking on autonomy, we are talking on equality—you Americans understand equality. An equal approach to all natural communities." Stephen blinked. The words, while well spoken, and syntax were muddled. Words falling in place like leaves in a storm. Stephen could only stare dumbly.

Green Tie tugged at his comrade's sleeve. Milošević looked at him in puzzlement. Then he nodded in understanding. "Excuse me," he said to Stephen as the two Serbians rose simultaneously from the couch and stood facing him. "I wish you very good evening."

Then the third president of the Federal Republic of Yugoslavia and his apparatchik companion turned away from Stephen, who watched as they disappeared into the restaurant in search of tasty Serbian schnitzel.

The sun was just setting as he arrived at the studio. Stephen was momentarily mesmerized by the spectacular sky. Homer came to mind: *Rosy-fingered sunset.* He felt like Odysseus struggling to return to Ithaca but stuck on the island of Aeaea, the guest of the enchantress Circe. Stephen knew something about witches. But then, so did Marlowe: *Was this the face that launch'd a thousand ships?* Far from home. Strange lands. Mysterious cave. Lyrical sky. Beautiful women: Circe and Helen from the classics; Elaine, Diane, Biljana, Minerva from his own life.

As he stepped out of the car, he turned and offered his hand. Biljana grasped it and smiled. Standing next to him on the pavement outside the studio, she seemed momentarily lost, as if she'd forgotten where the entrance to the sound stage was located. She looked left and right, as if she'd misplaced a shoe in the darkness of a bedroom.

"Are you hungry?" he offered, resting his hand on her shoulder to ground her.

"*Hong*ry?" intoned Biljana, shaking her head, smiling nervously.

He mimed eating food, like Charlie Chaplain in *The Gold Rush* (or maybe it was *The Kid*?), grasping an invisible spoon and rapidly shoveling air into his mouth. He realized how ridiculous this must have looked to Lorenzo, who shook his head in disgust as he passed them on his way to the set.

"The Jelovnik Restorana Žabar is *family restaurant*," said the First A.D. when Stephen asked him for a recommendation. "You go there." But then he glared at Biljana disapprovingly; she is, after all, a lowly set decorator, while Stephen is the director. There are certain matters of etiquette to be followed on a movie production.

"*Nalazi se na reci,*" he continued, frowning. "It is on the river."

Stephen thought: a restaurant on a boat docked along the riverbank. What could be more romantic? On the Danube, no less.

"Specialty is Morska riba," the A.D. insisted while eyeing Biljana with a look of contempt.

− 41 −

Zivko dutifully drove them to the restaurant. (In the past two days, he'd made no mention of the demonstration or of Stephen's disappearance.) On the way they passed the Hotel Jugoslavija. The name on the front of the building was colossal in size.

"*Jedan od najstarijih luksuznih srpskih hotela,*" said Biljana. She was sitting in the passenger seat in front, Stephen in the back.

Zivko turned to look at Stephen. "She said is oldest luxury hotel in Belgrade." His gaze quickly returned to the road ahead as a car cut him off. He swerved to avoid collision, tires squealing.

Stephen thought for a moment. He'd heard the name of this hotel before. Not because famous celebrities had stayed there—Richard Nixon, Tina Turner, Buzz Aldrin. Not because it housed the biggest chandelier in the world, which was a source of pride in Belgrade. Rather, because it was Buckfellow's hotel. Crew rumors had it that the star chose to stay at this hotel rather than the one housing the rest of the actors and Italian crew—Stephen's hotel—because he coveted his privacy. Apparently Buckfellow, a married man, would take his sexual conquests—and there were many of them, the rumors suggested—back to his hotel after a day's shoot. The hotel staff were famously discreet.

While they were only rumors, the story rang true.

The dining room was almost empty. It was early for dinner, by Belgrade standards—six o'clock. "The city that never sleeps," the guidebooks boast. Not in the guidebook but known to everyone: White City. Sin City. The Las Vegas of Eastern Europe.

It was a somewhat rustic-looking place, the restaurant. Its wooden elements gave it a warmth and charm that pleased Stephen. His eyes moved. There was a view of the river from their table through big plate glass windows—the murky river, a section of the sky, clouded but still glowing. He watched other tables being set for dinner. A few elegant patrons were beginning to arrive, well dressed, two men pulling out chairs for women as they moved to sit. Men wearing jackets and ties, women with pearl necklaces. He was used to L.A.: ever casual, T-shirts and Levi's, gym shorts or sweat pants, sometimes bathing suits, even miles from the beach.

Stephen and Biljana were casually dressed. His blue jeans, sweatshirt, and down jacket, as always; her ethnic dress, horribly out of place. She did not seem aware of the anomaly nor uncomfortable, though. She ignored her surroundings. Instead, she focused all her attention on Stephen, displaying that beautiful slow smile of hers, those crimson lips.

They studied their menus in silence. Stephen could not read a word and stared dumbly at it. When he arrived at their table, the waiter sensed that Biljana would do the talking; it was probably Stephen's ludicrous western clothing, and so he turned to her rather than Stephen. She ordered for both of them, dishes that sounded to him like gibberish.

The waiter left. She laughed nervously, a high laugh. They did not know what to say or do. They scrutinized each other's faces in silence. Hers was striking in its exoticness, her Dinaric ethnicity, Stephen decided. Was it the makeup? The high cheekbones? Broad face? Light eyes? Her hair had been bleached blonde, but not recently; he could see the black roots. Her flaws did not matter. She possessed an abundantly exotic, exquisitely feminine sexuality. She was a goddess, he thought. Was it Helen? Or was it Aphrodite? No, Circe.

She was seized with a sudden merriment:

"*Imaš divno lice*," she said, reaching across the table and touching his cheek. You have a wonderful face.

Stephen looked confused. "Sorry. I don't speak Serbian. Um … *ja ne goverim srpskih.* I wish I did. Now more than ever."

"*Nije bitno. Oči govore tečno.*" It does not matter. Your eyes speak fluently.

To Stephen, her words were utterly incomprehensible, but she spoke them with such kindness in her tone that

Stephen held his breath. He then coughed, a jitterbug sputtering, and they both laughed.

"*Izvinjavam se,*" Stephen apologized—sorry. It was one of a half-dozen Serbian words he'd needed to learn.

"*To je u redu,*" she breathed, her voice growing husky. It's okay. "*Razumem te.*" I understand you.

She placed her left elbow on the table, rested her chin on her palm, and gazed intently at him. It was then that he noticed the small white circle of flesh around the finger. She'd recently removed her wedding ring, it seemed.

"Your finger." He mimed twisting his own outstretched finger of his left hand. "You're married?"

At first perplexed, she looked at her finger. Then she placed her ringless hand in her lap. Her eyes flitted first left, then right. Lost something again. Suddenly nervous. Then she looked straight at him, with conviction.

"Ieee? … haaave? … boyfrrrrriend?" Was she asking a question? he wondered. She then looked down at her lap.

Stephen decided not to pry further. "Never mind. It's all good. *Dobro.*"

Then her eyes met his. "*Da, ali ne razumete. Un dečko. Imam dečka. On je kapetan policije,*" she said, speaking quickly. Yes, but you do not understand. I have a boyfriend. He is a police captain.

Stephen stared blankly, failing to comprehend. Then: "Your husband?" he asked with urgency. He made the gesture of twisting his ring finger once more. "*Husband?*"—a little too loudly. Patrons turning to look.

"No, no, no," she said rapidly. "Not *muž*. He … eeeze

… onlee … ah … *boyfrrrend.*" And she added brightly: "Eeeeze … *hokay.*" She nodded resolutely to cement the reassurance.

He wanted to believe her, so he did. It would be okay.

The meal was delicious. *Foie gras pâté, hobotnica sa pistaćima, morska riba,* and *sa vrganjima,* concluding with *sezonske salate.* Dessert of *cokoladni kolac* and a bottle of Vinarija Zvonko Bogdan wine. They rarely spoke while they ate. Much was communicated with the eyes alone. Like one of the earliest hominins, they walked on two legs, Stephen and Biljana, but how would they communicate? Like Stone Age Neanderthals? Grunts, scratching, pointing, squealing?

What Stephen and Biljana expressed to each other was primordial.

The bill came to 1,430,000 dinars. *One million!* he thought as he stared horrified at the check. He had no idea what this came to in dollars. He shrugged it off. Carpe diem. He paid with his wife's Wells Fargo credit card, which he'd borrowed from her for emergencies. *This an emergency! But what will I tell Elaine when the statement comes in the mail?* he wondered. Dinner for two—for him and his director of photography or the production manager, he'd say. To celebrate the conclusion of principal photography. Elaine would not be angry with him, as he'd accumulated a great deal of per diem money, more than enough to compensate for the credit card expense. Not to mention the fee for directing. She would be pleased. There would be no quarreling. There would be only celebration.

That was when it hit him. He hadn't spoken to Elaine in three days.

– 42 –

The evening had only begun.

They flagged down a cab outside the restaurant and climbed in. It took them to the center of Belgrade, to Rajićeva 10.

There was a crowd in front of the *Klub Akademija*. The cab driver explained:

"Oldest club in Beôgrad. Now eeeze in building of Facul-teee of Fieeene Harts. Eeeze cent-tar ef avant-garde," he told Stephen. "All big eeemportant bands. V-I-A Talas, Deesipleen Spi-eeen. EKV, Blok — great bands!"

Stephen paid the driver, singling out the big notes, and they got out. Biljana led Stephen by the hand, guiding him in a zigzag pattern through the crowd. Stephen decided it was necessary to adopt a Zen Buddhist mind-set in order to navigate these surroundings: rowdy, engulfing him. He conjured up in his mind the image of a blooming lilac. Light purple flowers in thick clusters. Peace, calm. Peace, calm …

They made their way to the front where two bouncers blocked their path. One was scowling; he had a face like a

moonscape: pockmarked. The other was a bulky, towering
man, a dark giant. Two young thugs.

"*Oni djeluju kao tampon između montenegrina i srbijanaca,*"
explained Biljana. The bouncers are a buffer between Mon-
tenegrins and the local Serbs.

"What?" he said, not comprehending. "*What?*"

"*Montenegrina!*" she shouted. Then she shook her head,
giving in to hopelessness. "No mind!"

The bouncers seemed to know Biljana; they smiled
knowingly at her. She smiled back flirtatiously. It bothered
Stephen, these knowing grins, suddenly feeling possessive.
She'd been here before. Were there other men? Of course! he
figured; she is beautiful. The thugs waved her and Stephen
through.

Inside, the music of EKV—Ekatarina Velika—blasted
from speakers. Stephen winced as the high volume felt
like hypodermic needles being driven into his brain. Biljana leaned close and shouted that Milan Mlademovic,
the band's lead singer, was singing (wailing in Stephen's
pained opinion) about fleeing his boring life for distant,
entertaining Amerika, so far far away. Stephen understood
not a word she spoke.

Cement walls enclosed them on all sides, arches adorned
with black and white graffiti, skull shapes. Stephen spotted
a stone sculpture of a woman, tall and thin like a Giacometti
but with a pregnant belly. Green light strobing on the walls,
a disco ball overhead. No one was sitting at the small round
tables that dotted the dance floor. They were all standing,
swaying, dancing, like one pulsating organism. The dance

floor was packed with pierced youth, some with their hair spiked, lips painted black, shouting—no, bleating, thought Stephen, like lambs to the slaughter; no, shrieking like harpies in a Ray Harryhausen flick. This was the gathering place for Gothic, darkers, punks, Satanists, lunatics—they were all there that night, the youth of Yugoslavia, facing civil war, mad for change.

Stephen took it all in. Jostled by bodies on all sides. Deafening music. A lack of air. Stephen could smell the stink of armpits. He was beginning to feel giddy, nauseous.

"Can I get you a drink?" Stephen shouted at Biljana, thinking that numbing alcohol would help. Biljana gave him a puzzled look. He mimed chugging down a shot.

"Da! Da!" she yelled.

"Okay. What're you having?"

"Hav—ink?"

"Drinking. *What?*"—fleeting annoyance. The music's volume, an accumulation of frustration. It was becoming too much.

"Oh! *What*! I … want … Rakia!"

He nodded and slowly made his way to the bar, still clutching her hand, leading her there, afraid to let her go. Getting lost in this place would be hell.

He managed to get the bartender's attention after ten minutes of waving his arms. When the rakia finally came, and after Stephen paid with a tall stacked monolith of banknotes mined from his pocket, Biljana and Stephen clinked glasses together and drank the stuff down in one painful gulp. His eyes watered; she seemed unfazed. Apri-

220   Jeffrey Kwitny

cots, thought Stephen, the taste erasing any remnants of lilac from his consciousness. It reminded him of Italian grappa. Pure firewater.

In no time his head was reeling. Soon they drank two more rakias each, and danced. Stephen moved his body in spasmodic jerks, imitating the others as best he could, feeling no pain, lost in an alcoholic trance. The drinks had crept up on him like a mugger and hit hard. At least his migraines were kept at bay.

A loud bang cut through the din, like a baseball bat smacking a table. The more sober patrons looked up in confusion, startled. It was a gunshot, not a baseball bat. Women and men began shouting, a few screaming.

"What? What?" shouted Stephen at Biljana in bewilderment, hoping she could explain. They'd stopped dancing and looked around. She shook her head, eyes worried.

The mass of dancers began to move en masse toward the exit doors, as if a fox had just entered the henhouse. Drunken chickens flapping their wings, clucking, and colliding into each other, moving toward the only exit.

Biljana leaned into Stephen, bringing her mouth up to his ear.

"Eeees a *pištolj*!"

Oh shit, he thought.

"Theyeee … sayeee … weee … go," she explained. Stephen nodded and followed closely behind her as she struggled to move forward. Bodies around them moved as one. Stephen could hear laughter blending with sporadic screams—a night of fun.

And then they found themselves outside the club, and the shock of cold air was sobering. It was like coming out of a dark multiplex theater after watching two movies—they were jolted back to reality. And reality was chaos. Patrons fanned out in all directions around them, some running, some stumbling, some dazed and motionless, others frightened and visibly agitated.

Biljana began to laugh. Stephen loved the sight of her white teeth, her body shaking with mirth. He laughed too, although he had no idea why.

"Eees *ho*-kay!" she reassured him, snickering hiccups. Stephen pulled her to him and wrapped his arms about her protectively. She snorted into his collar as her laughter died down. She seemed to fold into Stephen, he thought, like egg whites into cake batter.

She suddenly pulled away from him and took his hand in hers. She looked into his eyes, then she turned and led him away. Stephen experienced euphoria: to be walking with this mesmerizing, almost unbearably beautiful woman, hand in hand …

They disappeared into the cover of darkness.

Stephen looked skyward. Straight overhead, as if on cue, as if in a movie, a phalanx of meteorites streaked downward like falling spirits, bright against the black dome of sky, then quickly vanished. Stephen knew from his studies at Cal about the myths. Asteria, the goddess of falling stars. The Greeks saw them as portentous signs.

He was too distracted to read them.

•   •   •

Even outside in the cold night air, everything was out of focus. He was drunker than he thought. He was not sure how they got there. They were standing in an alley now, far from noisy Kneza Mihaila. Stephen could not hear the sound of traffic; he could only hear the sound of blood pounding in his ears.

Biljana was leaning against a wall, first with her left arm then turning to her back. His first thought was that she was tired, but her eyes were bright, even in the darkness, and she was giggling, bringing both her hands up to her mouth, the way some people do out of politeness when they are talking while chewing food. There was a rain gutter drainpipe extending from the roof to the ground, flanking her like an extended exclamation point on one side, and a trash bin, on the other.

He went quickly to her. Lips joined lips. Her arms went around his neck. He responded by placing his hands around her waist, and he held her tight as if he feared she'd pull away. Then his hands moved lower, and he pressed his hips hard against her. They continued with the kiss, heads twisting, tongues delving, hips pressing. Clothing kept blocking. He was in a kind of delirium, wanting to be transported away from himself, from this alley, from Yugoslavia, from the known world. To be spirited away, spirit rather than matter, moving heavenward …

Then he stepped back, as if awakening from a dream. He blinked. His vision began to clear.

"What am I doing? What the hell am I doing!!" He sounded like a madman.

And then she, still propped against the wall, stepped abruptly aside, away from him, cut like a severed artery, blood fading from her cheeks. Stephen stood dazed, still blinking rapidly, looking around as if a sideshow hypnotist had just snapped his fingers, breaking the trance.

"What is wrong with me?" he said, turning his face away from her. "I can't do this." He cupped his face in his hands.

She stared, bewildered at first. Then she smiled. There was even a subtle look of relief that crossed her face.

"*Postaje kasno*," she said huskily, still a bit aroused. It is getting late. "*Vreme je da idemo kući, ljubavi moja.*" Time to go home, my love.

– 43 –

The cab dropped him off at his hotel. He gave the driver enough dinars to cover his fare and later Biljana's. As the cab began to pull away from the curb, she waved to him from the back seat, smiling, those bright teeth of hers, Cheshire cat–like in the darkness of the cab interior. The taxi disappeared into the brooding city.

Once inside the hotel, Stephen scanned the lobby but saw no one. It was late. The rest of the crew was long asleep.

The clerk behind the desk—always the same tired, balding, cynical man, never anyone else—called out to Stephen as he made his way toward the stairs:

"Meeester Krawczyk."

Stephen stopped, turned.

"Please, sir," the man said, beckoning to him, waving a hand.

Stephen walked to the front desk.

"Please, sir," he repeated deferentially. "You have message." He handed Stephen a small folded piece of paper. "Your vife kalled."

Opening the note, he read the words: STEPHEN. CALL HOME. ELAINE. 17.03.

She'd called hours ago, around dinner time in L.A.

He jotted his home number on a hotel notepad and gave it to the clerk. He sprinted to the phone booth. Once inside, he swiveled the door closed and lifted the phone from its cradle. He waited for the call to go through. Adrenalin fueled, his mind was sharp. Sweat on his brow. Then a tinny voice emitted from the earpiece:

"Hello!"—her voice strident.

"Ellie. It's Stephen. What's going on?" He held his breath.

"Oh, Stephen. I tried to call you yesterday. You didn't get my message?"

"You did? Yesterday?" He tried to remember what he was doing the night before. Why hadn't he gotten the message? He was feeling displaced in time. "Uh, no. No one told me. It's been … crazy. What's wrong?"

"Remember those crank calls? That nutcase I told you kept calling?"

"Yeah, yeah, what—"

"He finally talked to me. He said … he said he's going to kidnap our daughter."

It took a few beats for the horror to sink in. "Are you sure?" said Stephen. "He said that?"

"He threatened to kidnap Em," she said, hardening her voice against the challenge.

"*What the hell*?"—growing outrage, Stephen's face reddening with anger.

"I know. Scared the crap out of me."

"What'd he say, *exactly*?"

"He just said 'Better keep an eye on your daughter. She might disappear one day.' That's it. All he said. He hung up before I could ask questions." And then she added: "I thought I heard a woman snickering in the background. I don't know. Could've been another man."

"Ellie, what … did you call the police?" He was now shouting into the phone. His heart was racing. He gripped the phone tighter. He felt completely helpless. "Damnit!" He smashed the flat of his free hand against the glass door, rattling it. The clerk behind the desk looked up, alarmed. Stephen met his stare, shook his head.

"Stephen. It's all right," she said soothingly. "I've got it under control. I called the police, and they gave me the number for the FBI." She sounded eerily relaxed, her speech almost normal. But this was like Elaine, Stephen thought. Pull it together in emergencies. Take control. She was always the grownup, he the child.

"Are you kidding? The FBI?" *Holy Christ*, he thought.

"Some guy with a very flat voice. I wrote his name down somewhere. Agent Something-or-Other. He sounded almost bored, like a bureaucrat. But he took my call seriously, wrote down what I said. Then they tapped our phone."

"They came to the apartment," he stated in disbelief.

"No. They did it from their end, I guess."

Stephen stood up straight, eyes wide. "Wait a minute. The phone's tapped? Right now? They're listening *now*?" So the Belgrade police would also be listening in, he realized. Was the world in on the call?

"I *guess*. They said they're waiting for the guy to call again. So they can trace the call?" she asked. She had little interest in technology and relied on her filmmaker husband to explain those things. "He told me to signal to them when he calls back."

"What do you mean?"

"Just say, 'Why are you threatening me?' when he's on the line. Like I said, he hasn't called since the last time."

Stephen ran his fingers through his hair, turning left and then right in the tight space of the booth, as if looking futilely for an escape. *It could only be Colon. Yes. He would do this. Exactly the sort of goddamned creepy thing he'd do. To get me to leave the production, leaving it for Trueblood to finish.* They'd warned Stephen about the producer. Everybody had. He'd ignored the warnings. But then, why didn't they just fire him? It made no sense, he figured. Because they knew he wouldn't leave the studio without a fight. Because they were sick people. Because Colon was a snake. Because he'd fallen into a pit of vipers. Because he was a fool.

"Did he have a British accent?" he asked.

"No, um, no he didn't. I don't think so, anyway."

Colon could've put anyone up to making the call for him, reasoned Stephen; there are a thousand sycophants at Starlight, in the film business. And Colon would be shrewd enough to avoid speaking himself, with that distinctive voice of his. Or he could have faked an American accent.

"Okay," Stephen said, struggling to stay calm. "When did the guy call?"

"Yesterday morning. I called your hotel right after."

"And he hasn't called since?"

"No. Not yet."

Stephen thought carefully. How much time had he wasted since yesterday morning? How far had he fallen off a cliff?

"Elaine. You've got to take Em somewhere safe."

"Yes. I know. I called my brother in Ojai. I know, we haven't talked in a while. But I asked. He's happy to help. Nobody knows where he lives, or even that I have a brother, so it's perfect. The agent thought that was a good idea."

"It *is*. Good. Your crazy brother Ted."

"Crazy Brother is going to help."

"Well, that works. For now."

"We were about to leave when you called."

Oh God. If I'd called later, nobody would've picked up. Except maybe an FBI agent.

"I'll call you from his place," she continued. He was silent. "We'll be all right, Stephen. The FBI guy said for us to leave. But they'll keep us safe."

"No," said Stephen definitively.

"No? No what?"

"I'm coming home. I have to be there."

"Stephen! What about your movie? Are you finished?"

"We have a few scenes left to shoot—" And there were still weeks of post-production work in Rome: pickup shots, special effects, editing, scoring. At least another month. He'd only received the first third of his salary.

"Then stay and finish it, Stephen. We'll be *okay*."

With Elaine in charge, they probably would be fine, he reasoned. But what then? Stay at Uncle Ted's? For how long? Until what? And what else might Colon do?

They needed him. His family needed him.

"To hell with the movie," he said definitively. "I'm coming home"—stated with utter resoluteness. "I gain a day on the flight. I'll leave tonight, be home tomorrow."

There was a long pause. Then: "Okay." There was sadness in her voice.

"Wait for me at the apartment. I'll drive you to your brother's. We'll all go together."

It was strange. He felt helpless, being so far away from home, and yet a new boundless energy filled him all the same. Once home, he would make sure Em and Elaine were safe.

And then he would track down Colon and break his neck.

– 44 –

He felt dirty. So he showered, hoping to wash away all traces of the night before. The water went suddenly cold, and he twisted the hot and cold handles back and forth feverishly, desperately, but then he gave up. He stepped out from behind the curtain, shivering, and reached for the towel he'd placed on the toilet seat. He dried himself and reached for his T-shirt and boxer shorts.

He set his alarm for 5 a.m. and turned off the light on the bedside table. He climbed into bed, sliding under the stiff sheet, and pulled the blanket up to his chin.

It was impossible to fall asleep. Adrenalin flowed in his veins and would not abate. His heart was still pumping rapidly. He laid there thinking. His mind was acutely alive, running through possibilities, the future, sorting out ... He would fly home tomorrow night, after the day's shoot: the big final scene. It was the last important shoot of the production, and he would get it done. Nobody would shoot that scene but him—the *climax*, as Borko would say, hands waving extravagantly in the air. To hell with the cave, the school exteriors, post-production work in Rome. They did not need him. Trueblood could cut the film anyway he liked.

He began making a list in his head, a checklist for later today. He would

- ✓ wake up at 5:00 a.m. and book a flight out of Belgrade Airport;
- ✓ finish shooting the last important scene of his movie;
- ✓ have Zivko drive him to the airport, then catch his flight out;
- ✓ drive to the apartment from LAX;
- ✓ hug and kiss Elaine and Em, and tell them how much he loved them;
- ✓ drive them to her brother's place, get them situated there;
- ✓ deal with Colon;
- ✓ confess everything to Elaine, cry his heart out, ask for absolution;
- ✓ take care of his beloved wife and stepdaughter, and
- ✓ be good and true from then on.

That was the plan.

He thought about this list as he stared at the ceiling. He kept thinking about Elaine and Emily, and he thought of Biljana too, and Minerva, although he tried not to—until the alarm shattered the silence and drove him into action.

– 45 –

The concierge made the arrangements. There was a flight out that night on Aeroflot, leaving BEG airport at 11:35 p.m. and arriving at LAX at 1:50 p.m. on Sunday. The fare was 1,591 U.S. This was not a problem; he would have been on that plane at any cost. He paid with the Wells Fargo card, dictating the account number and expiration date over the phone.

Zivko was oddly silent and solemn on the drive to the studio. Stephen tried to goad him into conversation by asking him what he did the night before. His one-word response—"sleep"—was unsettling, out of character for this normally gregarious and vociferous young man.

Another bad omen, thought Stephen.

Stephen decided not to say anything further and sat silently in the passenger seat staring out the window, watching the gray buildings pass by. There was the Ikarus building, once the administrative building of a long-defunct aircraft factory. One of the oldest preserved buildings in

New Belgrade. Pure Art Deco. A thing of beauty, thought Stephen, a little sadly.

– 46 –

When they arrived at the studio, he flung open the door, leaped out, the car still rolling to a stop, and then sprinted to the building's front door. Once inside, he walked briskly down the hall to Stage 4. He found the door to the sound stage closed tightly. An amiable young man, someone Stephen had not seen before, stood at the door, blocking Stephen from entering.

"*Mi dispiace, signore, non puoi entrare,*" the man said.

"What?"

"*Scuse.* I ... am ... *afraid* you ... are *not*-a ... all*ow*ed to enter*rr*, sign*ore.*" Was he from Rome? Stephen wondered. He had an L.A.-style David Hasselhoff haircut, preppy clothes. *Who is this guy?* Driven by fury, Stephen swept the young man aside roughly with an arm and opened the door.

Inside the stage, he stopped, closed the door behind him quietly, and surveyed the interior from the back. The crew was in the midst of a shot. Lorenzo was hunched over the camera peering through the viewfinder, the lights were blazing, the actresses—completely naked and painted chalk-white—were standing on their marks.

Trueblood was wearing a ridiculous beret on his head. His hands were clasped behind his back in a commanding posture, chin and chest puffed out, in a pose recalling Il Duce. He said, in a soft voice yet loud enough in the silence of the space to be heard by all:

"*Tutti pronti*?" Then he repeated, in English: "Is everyone ready?"

Stephen spotted Borko off to the side in the back. He caught the manager's eye, and the big man lurched forward in his direction, walking on the balls of his feet to curtail sound.

"I guess I'm late," Stephen said, whispering. "I apologize."

"You're not late, my friend," said Borko, "because this man ..."—pointing at Trueblood—"has been shooting 'The Climax' ..."—he used air quotes—"since the day we left for the cave." He was grinning ruefully—idiot-faced.

Stephen froze.

"Borko! *He's* directing?"—tilting his head toward Trueblood.

"For that day. And now, since four this morning," he explained.

"Why didn't anyone—"

"Because you were not supposed to know," he replied, looking sheepishly down at his feet, then at Stephen. His expression was furtive. His once-friendly eyes now stared implacably at Stephen. "I am very sorry, Mister Stephen."

Stephen thought about this and gave Borko a withering look. "You knew all the time. While we drove to hell and back. Crawled around in that godawful cave. And then the day of the demonstration. I was gone all day. You knew all along!" Stephen leaned in to Borko: "Tell me, Borko: why didn't you say something?"

"I am ... terrible ..." —correcting himself—"*terribly* ... sorry—"

"So. That's how it's done. There's nothing else—"

"Please. I am just doing my job."

"*Trust me,* you said!" —Stephen, jaw clenching shut. He was staring now at his former ally with a look of unmitigated hatred. "You asshole," he growled.

"You can stay and watch ..." —feebly, again the idiotic grin.

"I can watch? *I can*—" Heat rising to his face quickly. Stephen could hardly speak. He'd entered some unfamiliar, strange state of being. Shock, injustice, massive betrayal. He might as well have been hit on the back of the head with a shovel. He felt a loathing choke him. But then he found his voice:

"My *masterpiece,* right, Borko?" Stephen said evenly, a final dig, now smiling oddly.

"Action!" called out Trueblood, apparently unaware of Stephen's presence at the back of the stage. The actresses, all fanged vampires, bright-red Karo syrup glistening on their chins, lips and breasts, let out a frightening wailing sound, a horrific screech, that filled the sound stage space.

Stephen's first thought was to race toward Trueblood, maniacally crying out "Cut!" But then a surprising calm came over him.

"Fuck this," he said, voice drowned out by the cacophony on the set, as he turned to the door, slamming it behind him as he left.

The young man standing at guard looked at him. "You *leave*-a?"

"I *leave*-a," said Stephen with finality. He walked out of Avala Studios into the winter light. He knew he'd never go back.

He signaled to Zivko, who was leaning with his elbow on the car and smoking a cigarette.

"Take me to the hotel," Stephen ordered.

As they drove off, Stephen took a last look at the studio building as it receded into the distance.

"*Arrivederci, Belgrado,*" he said softly, employing his best Italian accent.

− 47 −

As they pulled up to the curb in front of the Obrenović, with its façade of overscaled details, deep cornices, threadbare swags, and arcane sculptural elements, Stephen knew this would be the last time he stepped into this old hotel, his home for nearly a month.

"Wait in front. Back in ten minutes."

"Hokay. I will park in taxi lane," replied Zivko, who watched as Stephen flew out of the car and disappeared into the hotel.

"Oh, Meeester Krawczyk," said the clerk behind the desk. "You have phone call."

Stephen stopped on his way to the stairs, surprised. Who would be calling? Elaine? It's the middle of the night at home. Biljana? No, not a chance. she would not. Borko, to apologize and call him back? Unlikely. And how in hell would anyone know he was just now walking into the hotel? Was it a colossal coincidence? What were the chances of that? Was he being watched? The clerk appeared just as surprised as Stephen.

He walked over to the desk and took the phone that the clerk extended on its cord out to him. He placed the phone to his ear with trepidation.

"Hello?"

"Hello? Mister Krawczyk?" —it was a man's cheery voice, with just the faintest Serbian accent.

"Who is this?" said Stephen, heart pounding.

"I am Spiridon," the stranger replied.

Stephen waited.

"I am a good friend of Captain Đorđević of the Belgrade Police Department," he went on, speaking in a friendly, non-threatening voice, as if he were a long-lost relative calling from Stephen's past.

Stephen stood there petrified, full-blown panic kicking in, listening with a heightened sense of hearing. *All* senses on alert.

"The captain asked me to speak for him, his English is not so good," the man said.

"Okay. What does he want?" said Stephen, breathing faster, fighting to stay calm.

"It is not serious. Do not worry. The captain wants you to know that everything is all right."

"I don't understand."

"He wants you to know that it is okay for you to spend time with Biljana, the captain's girlfriend."

"What?" —heart racing. "Hold on. She's just a *friend*," pleaded Stephen.

"No! It is okay." the man insisted. "You can be with her. You have the captain's permission."

Stephen handed the phone back to the clerk, who gave him a bewildered look.

"Sir?" said the clerk, taking the phone, unsure what to do with it.

Stephen did not reply. He walked quickly across the lobby, passed the phone booths, then bounded up the stairway, feet landing on every other step. When he reached the fourth floor, he stopped to catch his breath. Bent over, hands on knees, breathing hard. But only for a moment. He stood upright and sprinted to his room.

Everything continued to happen fast. The key went into the slot, he turned the knob, pushed hard, the door flew open. He stepped inside and quickly closed the door, struggling to calm himself, closing his eyes, breathing deeply. He then turned and looked around the room and—

He immediately spotted the bright-white powder. It had been sprinkled by someone over the pillow, strewn on the bed and across the floor. He took a step to the bed and stared hard at the powder. He hoped to God it was talcum powder or some kind of cleaning agent, left by a rabid maid. He bent over and wetted a fingertip with his tongue. He dipped the finger into the powder and brought it to his lips, tasted it. A bitter flavor and slightly pungent smell. Like a mix of baking soda and rubbing alcohol.

Stephen knew instantly what it was: cocaine.

A police plant was the first thing that came to mind.

It wasn't enough that Captain Đorđević wanted to send a message to Stephen: stay away from Biljana. He wanted the randy American in jail—jail in a Communist country. A collapsing Communist country.

"Oh, shit," he said quietly. Then mounting hysteria. "Shit shit shit SHIT."

And then he saw the brick-sized package on the side table. Stephen took it in his hands and squeezed. It was soft, pliant; the wrapping paper crackled. He tore open a corner, and more white powder spilled out, snowfall at Mammoth Mountain, adding to the mess on the floor. Stephen looked toward the bathroom but knew his situation was hopeless. Even if he could flush much of the coke down the toilet, there would remain traces of it on the bed and carpet; he would need a vacuum cleaner. Where would he get that? And even then …

He quickly went for his suitcase, which was lying propped up and open against a wall. He did not bother with his toothbrush in a water glass or any clothes he may have left in the bathroom. His earnings, other than what remained in his wallet, were tucked away in a zipped-closed compartment within the suitcase. He checked it. Still there: lots. Dinar and dollars—one-third of his directing fee paid with a production company check, two thousand dollars of it paid when he arrived, the rest in dollars—thirty-three hundred dollars total; per diem money: three hundred dollars per week for four weeks, paid in dinar. It was still there, all of it.

He took out five one-hundred-dollar bills and placed

them in his wallet, crammed a roll of dinar into a pocket, and zipped the wallet inside a jacket pocket. He patted his jacket with both hands. His passport was still there, the inside pocket; so were the visa and a letter from the hotel Borko had acquired for him through the production company. He never went anywhere without them.

Cash, credit card, passport, visa, letter from the hotel—weapons of battle. He was ready.

He closed the bag, zipped it, crossed over to the door and opened it, shutting it quietly behind him as he left. He walked quickly down the hall to the stairway, a power walk—running would make too much noise, call attention to himself.

As he descended the stairs, he thought of the man at the front desk. There was the bill still to be paid. The production company would cover the hotel fees, he assumed, but he would be responsible for the phone calls. No matter. They had his wife's credit card on file.

When he arrived at the bottom of the stairs, Stephen turned to walk to the desk, but four men were talking to the concierge, their backs turned to Stephen. They were wearing blue pants, blue shirts, blue caps; weapons were strapped to their thighs.

Stephen stealthily turned a hard right and walked briskly into the restaurant at the rear of the lobby, then disappeared into the kitchen. He prayed to God he wasn't seen.

There would be a back door somewhere. He glanced around. Two men were working in the kitchen: elderly, tired, beaten down. One was stirring something in a large pot, the other was dicing carrots on a cutting board. They were mildly startled when Stephen entered the kitchen, but they'd seen too many tourists who'd lost their way before. Just another mixed-up foreigner. They looked more irritated than concerned.

"Door?" asked Stephen. "*Vrata*?"

The man making soup pointed to a corner of the kitchen. The door was behind a half-wall.

Stepping out into the alley, Stephen turned left without hesitation—he had a fifty-fifty chance that this was the shortest route—and began running in the direction of the busy street ahead. The stench of the alley—a sickening mixture of rotten eggs, animal feces, and moldy vegetables—assaulted his nose. He was aware that all his senses were heightened, fueled by adrenalin.

As he turned left on the busy boulevard, its sidewalk alive with pedestrians, he passed under a red awning that he hoped belonged to the hotel. The buildings in all other directions looked the same. He had no landmark points of reference. It would be easy to get lost—and to lose himself, for that matter—in this place. He spotted a closed Indian restaurant across the street, which he'd never noticed before.

When he came to the corner, he stopped. He did the movie trick of slowly peering around the corner of the building, hoping to avoid drawing attention to himself—used in every film noir movie ever made: *The Lady from Shanghai*, *Double Indemnity*, *Out of the Past*, *The Big Sleep* …

He was looking at the hotel entrance. There were no

policemen standing in front. By then, he imagined, they'd found his room empty and were rushing down the stairs. Maybe they would emerge from the hotel in a moment, guns unholstered. He hesitated. Was he overreacting? Had he seen too many movies? Maybe the police captain had been sincere in his friendliness. Just trying to be nice to the visiting American guest. Was Stephen simply being paranoid?

The powder on his bed was not spilt bathroom cleanser, a maid's clumsiness. No. The coke was real. *This* was real.

He spotted Zivko's white Yugo in the taxi zone. He hoped it was his, anyway; there were many white Yugos parked on this street. With great effort he walked toward the car as calmly as possible. When he finally stood on the curb alongside the vehicle, he bent down and peered through the passenger window. Zivko was sitting behind the wheel, eyes closed, head cocked to the side, mouth open, a trail of drool from the corner of his mouth to the edge of his chin.

Stephen tapped on the window. Zivko snapped awake, eyelids fluttering. Wiped his chin with the back of his sleeve. He looked over at Stephen, registered his face, and rolled down the window, looking flummoxed.

"Open the door, Zivko."

Shaking away his grogginess, Zivko unlocked the door obediently. Stephen flung the door open and climbed into the passenger seat, reaching back and placing his suitcase on the back seat.

"Drive me to the airport," he commanded, slamming the door shut.

Zivko looked doubtfully at Stephen, then at the suitcase.

"It's okay. I have money. I'll pay you," said Stephen, ignoring Zivko's worried look. "Let's go."

– 48 –

Belgrade's airport has a painful history. German occupation forces used the original one during World War II. The Allies bombed most of it in 1944. What they did not hit, the German army leveled while withdrawing from the country. Construction of the new airport began in 1958 and went on until 1962, when it was officially opened by Tito.

Steven and Zivko drove out of the city on the A3 motorway. They stopped at a toll station near the interchange close to the airport. Stephen handed Zivko a few dinar to cover it.

As they approached the airport, they could see plenty was amiss. The first thing they encountered was a traffic jam; cars were backed up for a mile. They waited. For some reason, cars were turning around and heading back toward them. They discovered why as they crawled ahead: the main artery leading into the airport was blocked.

A Yugoslav army tank stood in the middle of the road. A platoon of soldiers wearing camo uniforms and carrying semi-automatic firearms formed a second barrier in front of the tank. One of the soldiers was waving an arm in front of

him like a slow airplane propeller, indicating to the drivers
to turn their vehicles around.

"What's going on, Zivko?" asked Stephen with mounting dread.

"It happen," he said, amazed, eyes wide.

"What do you mean? *What* happened?"

"Finally happen, I tell you. I think is maybe revolution.
For real."

"They closed the airport?" It was a rhetorical question.
Oh, God …

"Looks like is so."

Stephen spoke quickly: "Can you get anything on the
radio?"

"Yes. Is good idea!"

Zivko turned on the radio while making a U-turn and
drove back the way they'd come. Stephen turned the radio
knob. All he could get at first was music. Something that
sounded to Stephen like a mixture of Caribbean and American jazz. He switched stations. Upbeat pop music this time
flooded the car interior.

"Is Nataš Gajović!" said Zivko jubilantly. "Is band
Zana!"

Stephen, grim-faced, turned the knob once more. A
news channel at last. Stephen listened intently, but the
Yugoslavian language—nothing but scattershot gibberish:

RADIO ANNOUNCER
*… nemiri su doveli do toga da je federalna vojska u kojoj
dominiraju Srbi zatražila vanredno stanje širom Jugoslavije …*

"Jebi ga!!" Zivko began screaming a string of epithets at the radio. He shook his head violently, as a dog shakes water from its fur after a bath.

"Zivko. What's going on?"

"He say unrest make federal army—army!—to wish? Invite? *Demand?*—state of emergency in all *Jugoslaviya*," explained Zivko, stumbling with the translation, fury giving way to deep concern.

RADIO ANNOUNCER
… Vojska namerava da sprovede kampanju za uspostavljanje reda u Beogradu …

"Military is to make ardor—order?" Zivko, struggling with the translation. "Orderly?—in Belgrade. Make not chaos." He angrily turned off the radio, burst into a brief polemic: "Is to defend country, not shut down airports! Anti-Communist protesters is what do this." He was beside himself. "Milošević do this."

Stephen was deep in thought as Zivko drove on, back to downtown Belgrade. Zivko would support the Communists—the status quo. He was making money, thriving in the black market. He had a decent enough job at Avala.

"What's the nearest international airport outside Yugoslavia?" he asked.

"Outside? What mean outside?"

"How far is Bucharest?"

Zivko turned to face Stephen, ashen faced, briefly taking his eyes off the road ahead. "Are you out of fooking mind?"

"How far is it?" Stephen repeated coolly.

Zivko stared at him. "Are you *luna-teeek*?" He shook his head dismissively, his eyes quickly returning to the road.

"You're probably right. I *am* insane, Zivko. *Beyond* insane. But then again, you're a smart businessman, right, Zivko? I'm a crazy American fool. So this is your opportunity. As we say in the great United States of America, a *golden* opportunity."

"I have job!" he said piteously. "At Avala Studio. *Za Boga miloga!*" For God's sake.

"How far?" Stephen repeated one more time, this time quite sternly.

"Hokay, hokay, let me think … I dunno. Maybe four, five hundred kilometers?"

"Not too bad, right? About how long you think?"

"Long?"

"*Time.*"

"Ah. Bucharest? Maybe, I dunno, three or four hours, something like that?"

"Fine. Just get me to the Romanian border, Zivko. I'll take it from there. That's, what, half the distance? You'll be back this afternoon. No one will know."

"Timișoara Airport is closer."

Stephen could almost hear the wheels turning in Zivko's mind: he would come up with some excuse for disappearing all day. There was money to be made. And it would be an act of defiance against the military.

"Is possible." Eyes looking upward as he made the calculation. "One hundred dollars U.S."

"One hundred!"

"Each way."

Stephen looked hard at him, then nodded in resignation, sitting back in his seat. No time to waste haggling price. Anyway, he'd spent—wasted?—a lot of money already. As long as he had enough to get home. Just get him the hell home.

He fished his wallet out of his pocket and plucked out a hundred-dollar bill. He handed it to Zivko.

"The rest when we get there," he said.

Zivko took it, and then pulled a cigarette out from his shirt pocket. Stephen watched as he dug a lighter out of the same pocket and lit up. It looked like a half-smoked joint, twisted and chewed.

"*Travu?*" said Zivko, offering it to Stephen. Weed?

Stephen shook his head. Not a chance. He needed it to be clear.

– 49 –

Zivko stopped only once, for gas. They drove in silence. The two-and-a-half-hour drive from the airport to the Romanian border sent Stephen tumbling into mental purgatory: a holding tank, awaiting judgment and leading to—hopefully—freedom. A fitting word, purgatory, for a fallen Catholic. For Stephen, home in L.A. would be heaven enough.

The Yugoslavian countryside flashed hypnotically before him, movie film unreeling at 24 frames per second.

"Villages dying," said Zivko mournfully, indicating a passing hamlet. "People they search for work in big cities—*Beǒgrad*. Is why I afraid lose job."

Stephen watched. A middle-aged man with a floppy hat and a long stick prodded a herd of sheep. Sitting down on a log an old man—eighty years old? a hundred?—and a child, maybe his granddaughter—twelve?—watched the traffic pass by, a table adorned with crimson peppers next to them. A woman, hair covered in a red scarf, seemed to be carrying a large bowl of—what were they, dead frogs?—to market. A muscular, sunburnt man with a pot belly shoed horses behind a fence.

"Is blacksmith," explained Zivko, shaking his head. "Few horses, though. See? Is little doing."

Stephen was looking out at the "ethno villages," picturesque hamlets scattered across the landscape, guardians of beloved traditions. Some of the houses looked like they were made of mud. Vineyards aplenty, a cornucopia of agricultural splendor, even a village famous throughout the world for red peppers. And the great gorges ... waterfalls ... mountain ranges ... hidden monasteries ... the place where sixteen Roman emperors were born. And monuments to the fallen fighters against fascism, a dozen at least, the bastard progeny of World War II.

What are our monuments at home? Stephen wondered. Stephen could picture L.A.'s landmarks vividly in his mind, he'd lived there much of his life: the Hollywood sign; Forest Lawn Cemetery; La Brea Tar Pits; the monolithic "Black Tower" at Universal Studios; Sleeping Beauty's castle at Disneyland; the white cliffside mansions of Malibu; the giant donut sign in Culver City; Watts Towers; Grauman's Chinese Theater; the Magic Castle in Hollywood; the great film studios and their spectacular facades and daunting signs: Paramount, Universal, Warner Bros., Disney, Twentieth Century Fox, Culver Studios ...

He was homesick. But none of that mattered. He would be home soon.

– 50 –

They would not take the route as Zivko had originally planned. The news on the radio reported that Romania had just closed some of its border crossings with Hungary and Yugoslavia: a military crackdown on demonstrators in the capital, Tirana, protesting the rule of hardline Communist leader Nicolae Ceaușescu was underway. Increased isolation imposed by the Communist regime; excessive militarization; surveillance and intimidation of local citizens—all this autocratic control would keep those areas outside the tourist circuit subdued for decades.

There were still road crossings at Moravița, Comloșu Mare, Jimbolia, and Porțile de Fier.

Zivko chose Moravița as their destination and took the E-70. It was a gamble, but it was the closest crossing and he was anxious to return to the studio.

With eighteen kilometers to go, they drove through the town of Vršac on the edge of the Pannonian Plain. Looking up,

Stephen sighted the Vršac Tower atop a great hill: Byzantine masonry, fifteenth century.

"A Monument of Culture of Great Importance!" said Zivko, elated and grinning.

It was to be the last monument in Yugoslavia Stephen would ever lay eyes on. Soon: the great monuments of Hollywood.

– 51 –

They arrived at the border in one-and-a-half hours.

"You give passport, registration card from hotel. And vignette, for Romania," said Zivko.

"A vignette? What's that?" said Stephen. He peered anxiously ahead out the window, looking for signs of the crossing station.

"More tax," sighed Zivko. He gave it some more thought. "No. Never mind. If you get ride with other person. *Other* guy pay. Is for *car*."

Then he muttered under his breath, like a curse: "*Poreza!*" Taxes and death, eternally reliable.

As they approached the crossing station, Stephen watched a green sign on the side of the road glide past, announcing: ВАТИН. "'Bath'?" Stephen asked. "They have like a bathhouse here, at a border crossing?" Zivko winced and corrected him: "Vatin. Serbian letters. It is where we are." Then they came to a halt behind a long line of stationary cars.

"They all go same way," said Zivko, slumping forward and hugging the wheel. It was a football field's distance to the station. "Everyone leaving."

"Doesn't matter," said Stephen, jumpy. "I'll make it." He felt utter fearlessness and resolution by now. Courage that comes on the heels of anxiety. He was beyond worried, feeling something feral, old as the living earth. He was fighting to protect his family.

"Here," he said, as he reached for his wallet inside his jacket. He took out another hundred-dollar bill and handed it to Zivko. Three left. "You'd better get back. Thanks for getting me this far."

Zivko gave him a worried look as he pocketed the bill, but the look was fleeting. He was happy to be rid of his American burden.

"Thanks for everything," said Stephen, meaning it, as he opened the door, stepped out of the car, reached for the back door handle, and opened it. He grabbed the handle of his suitcase—a smaller model, with wheels—and pulled it free. He leaned in to speak to Zivko:

"One last thing."

Zivko waited.

"What's the word for airport?"

"*Aerodrom*," said Zivko, smiling. It would be his last act of generosity with this visiting American movie director.

Stephen nodded, shut both doors, and watched Zivko pull out of the line of cars.

– 52 –

Two hours passed. Stephen had no luck catching a ride. People were already spooked by the military takeover, the airport closure; they dared not risk trouble by picking up this crazy American, this *ludi Amerikanac* in cowboy boots.

Then a massive thunderclap erupted as if out of nowhere. Spring is an unstable season in Yugoslavia. Mild periods alternate with the return of cold weather. Even late snowfalls can occur. It began to rain in buckets. Stephen was quickly drenched.

He looked up and down the long line of cars, vision blurred by rainwater. He blinked furiously. Despair began tugging aggressively at his coat sleeve like one of Romania's countless stray dogs, which were now everywhere in a country in decline.

He looked skyward. It looked like it had been mugged, taking on the color of a fresh bruise: black tinged with blue edges. He considered capitulating to the Fates and weeping.

The rain continued to beat down. Everything was working against him, it would seem. But he was a stubborn man, if nothing else, hellbent to return home.

Despite the gloominess and the pounding rainfall, despite humanity's giving him the cold shoulder, despite a sense of hopelessness that hounded him at every turn, Stephen nevertheless held onto a feeling something like optimism as he remembered: he was on his way home.

− 53 −

Nineteen eighty-nine was considered a golden year for Yugos; almost 200,000 of them were built that year in Yugoslavia, a country with a population of about 22 million. Red ones, blue ones, green ones, white ones slowly rolled forward, stopped, then continued on, passing him by. To the drivers watching him through their windshields he must have looked like a madman. He walked continuously up and down the line of cars in the rain, soaked to the bone, dragging behind him his suitcase rolling on its tiny wheels, bending down and peering inside the cars at the nervous passengers, repeating over and over:

"*Aerodrom*? *Aerodrom*?"

Then, finally, an arm and hand appeared, protruding through the window of one of the red ones, waving to him.

"Hey!" a disembodied voice called, and the hand gestured him over. When Stephen looked inside, he saw the passenger and the driver—both young men, perhaps in their early twenties—and one more of about the same age sitting in the back seat.

"Timișoara Airport—Aerodrom?" Stephen asked.

"Get in!" said the young man in the passenger seat triumphantly, his grinning face now close to Stephen's. He reminded Stephen of Ferris Bueller, played by Matthew Broderick, in the 1986 movie *Ferris Bueller's Day Off:* clean-cut, short hair, an endearing snaggle-toothed smile, sunglasses—All-American. Stephen looked over at the driver, and another 80s actor came to mind: Judd Nelson in *The Breakfast Club*. Good-looking kids, both, apparently having a good time, despite Yugoslavia's imploding.

The Ferris Bueller lookalike said "Excuse me" and opened the door as Stephen stepped back. The young man climbed out of the car and offered to take Stephen's suitcase and stow it in the trunk. "No room," he said as explanation, tilting his head toward the back seat.

Roosting there like a red Chanticleer, knees up to his chest and cradled by his arms, was a third young man. His bushy, crimson, Afro-style hairdo and celestial speckling of freckles across his cheeks reminded Stephen of Carrot Top, an American stand-up comedian and actor of the day. He waved to Stephen and smiled good naturedly. Stephen was beginning to feel something akin to relief. These were fellow Americans, such as they were. He could let his guard down at last.

Stephen handed his suitcase to Ferris, who walked behind the Yugo, opened the trunk, and wedged it carefully between three other suitcases. It was a tight fit, as the trunk was tiny.

Stephen then opened the back door and climbed in, settling in next to Carrot Top. He closed the door as Ferris got in, closing his door. The car remained stationary.

Stephen smiled uncomfortably. Awkward silence. Finally:

"Thanks, guys—for the ride."

Ferris, peering over the back of his seat at his guest admiringly, spoke first: "Honestly? You look pretty gnarly." It wasn't meant to be ironic; he meant it as a compliment. Disheveled, wet, eyes afire, Stephen looked like a character out of a wild and crazy road movie. Ferris chuckled and offered Stephen a high-five. Stephen reluctantly slapped his open hand against Ferris's, then wiped the water streaming down from his hair into his eyes with the back of a soggy sleeve.

"I'm Danny," said the young man in the front passenger seat.

"Stephen."

"I'm Alex, and I'll be your ticket out of this hellhole," said the driver: a good-looking kid with a Grecian nose, thick lips, and hair that swept like a wave across his forehead. With his relatively subdued demeanor, he seemed the oldest and wisest of the three, nodding his head and smiling as if acknowledging the Great Truth of what he'd said.

"Connor!" said the redhead sitting alongside Stephen, affably, still grinning, an expression that Stephen was beginning to think was etched permanently on his face.

Stephen sat motionless, eyes darting from one to the

other of them, their steady gazes bearing down on him out of curiosity. Feeling more uneasy by the moment, he broke the silence again.

"I take it you guys are on vacation."

"Spring break," explained Alex.

"If you like vacationing in Dante's *Inferno*," said Connor. "I mean, really? Are you kidding me? You ask me, Yugoslavian socialism sucks."

"Romania," piped in Alex in full professorial mode now, "is even worse. It's like this, only worse. Nicolae Ceaușescu heads the Romanian Communist party. An autocrat, right?—the worst. Romanians are, like, fighting for survival. Food rationing, electricity blackouts. All radio stations closed and—get this—TV limited to only two hours a day. Now that is fascism."

Danny dutifully explained: "Alex had to write a paper on Eastern Europe. Who the fuck majors in Eastern European history? *This* guy does!" he said, giving his friend a poke in the right bicep with an extended index finger. "I don't know, maybe because he's Jewish?"

"They're not fucking around here," Alex added, glaring at Danny. Then, directed at Stephen: "I mean, we're talking *genocide*."

Stephen winced. *Great. Out of the frying pan, into the fire.*

Alex looked back over his shoulder: "We have three days to get back to the States."

"*Major* hassle," groaned Connor.

Stephen: "Why three days?"

"Classes start," said Danny.

"We timed this whole thing wrong," said Alex. "But who knew?"

"This is *supposed* to be a vacation," opined Connor with an exaggerated grimace.

Stephen nodded, turning to Connor. "What college?"

"Arizona State, man. The Sun Devils!"

"We were pretty stoked," said Danny.

The driver took his foot off the brake and eased on the gas pedal; the car pulled forward a few yards. "Finally," he said. Then stopped the car.

Danny went on: "An Eastern European 'whirlwind extravaganza,' the ad said."

Alex: "Budapest, Belgrade, Warsaw, Prague—"

"Bucharest too, but we don't have time," Danny said sadly, shaking his head.

Connor looked at Stephen. "What about you?"

Stephen was looking out the window. Rain streaming down the glass in thick rivulets.

"Working on a movie," he replied softly, face still turned away. He immediately regretted it. The last thing he wanted to do was talk about the aborted production.

Danny: "Not even. Seriously?"

Stephen smiled weakly. He began to feel nauseous.

"What kind of movie?" Alex looked back ahead over the seat. The cars continued to inch forward. He eased the car up a few feet.

"A horror film." Stephen watched the rain on the glass blur the view, turning the world outside into an abstract expressionist painting mirroring his internal disjointed state.

The beginnings of another migraine were taking shape.

The three of them stared admiringly at Stephen.

Connor: "Saw the baddest flick ever. You see *Child's Play*?"

"No, *Die Hard*," argued Danny.

"That's not a horror flick, man," fired back Connor. Danny merely shrugged his shoulders.

Alex: "*Beetlejuice*, if you ask me. Great special effects."

Stephen clenched his eyes closed and remembered the VCR back in the hotel room. Zivko's pirated videocassettes. All a waste of money.

The car approached the gate. A guard stepped up to the window and Alex stopped the car. The three students and Stephen handed the man their documents.

The guard made demands. They would each have to produce one hundred U.S. dollars in cash, which must be spent in Romania, he instructed. They had no choice. They would have to change the currency at a nearby store, which had transformed itself into a thriving cottage industry overnight. One hundred dollars worth of Romanian *leu*.

Stephen sighed. He took stock. Ninety thousand Lions to pack into his pocket. He did the math quickly in his head. A company check for a thousand, another thousand in per diem in the suitcase. He had two hundred U.S. dollars left.

•   •   •

Stephen noted that the first striking difference between the two countries, Yugoslavia and Romania, was the condition of the highways. On the Serbs' side of the crossing, the asphalt was in decent condition. On the Romanians' side: unpaved roads. There were mounds of garbage, rusting factories, shacks without roofs, buildings in the distance that were equally neglected, left half-built, surreally incomplete. The air was sooty and murky, as the citizens burned soft coal 24 hours a day.

As they drove along the bumpy road, the driver/historian who looked like Judd Nelson told Stephen that according to his research, things would just disappear suddenly from stores with no explanation. "No onions. No cabbage. Ordinary stuff like pots and pans—even stupid stuff like coat hangers—all disappeared, like, in the blink of an eye."

Stephen thought about the apartment in Santa Monica. Despite their modest income, Stephen, Elaine, and Emily enjoyed all the basic creature comforts: Elaine always kept a cornucopia of fresh fruit and vegetables in a bowl in the little dining area; plenty of protein dishes—chicken, salmon—in the fridge. They had a Sony Bravia TV and a Commodore computer. They had a decent apartment, small as it was. An unfaltering stream of hot water and electricity. All in all, they lived a decent life in a thriving metropolis.

"I was sort of hoping we'd have time for Poenari Castle," said Danny, frowning in disappointment.

"The castle where Dracula supposedly lived," explained Alex, glancing back at Stephen for his reaction. Stephen was facing the window; his eyes were clenched closed now.

Hearing the name Dracula, Connor sat up straight,

brightening. "Vlad the Impaler! Now we're talkin' *real* horror."

"Ain't gonna happen," said Alex.

– 54 –

They stopped to eat, against Stephen's protestations; he was anxious to get to the airport. He was sick with anxiety and wasn't hungry.

It was a tiny place just off the highway, in a small village, a shoebox of a restaurant with its name hand-painted on a wall: **Небеска Храна.** Heavenly Food. A pack of snarling feral dogs circled the building.

Inside there were six small wooden tables. All but one were occupied. Stephen assumed the other patrons at this uninviting, dismal place were part of the exodus of people fleeing Serbia. People were lowering their faces toward bowls of gray, hesitantly spooning it into their mouths. The walls were hung with dirty drapes. There was an old faded portrait of Stalin on one wall and a tiny photograph of Ceaușescu on another. Another wall was plastered with copies of *Scînteia,* a Communist newspaper.

A figure wearing a designer sport jacket and crisp white shirt with the top button left undone, wavy gray hair—a distinguished-looking solitary man—was sitting at a table, his refinement oddly incompatible with the surroundings. He turned and watched the four Americans as they entered the restaurant.

Stephen and the three young men sat at a table. They ordered bowls of soup, a local specialty—"*fel de mâncare specială*," said the waiter, sporting bushy sideburns and smiling devilishly. He chuckled at an apparent inside joke. He placed four bowls and four bottled soft drinks in front of the Americans. They ate silently, morosely, stirring the broth with their spoons. Hot, brackish water with a few chunks of onion, potato, and carrot.

Turning in his chair to face the young men, the stranger said, paternally: "People here don't eat quite as well as they do in the States." He spoke with a faint German accent. "Usually it's bread and milk in the morning. A sandwich with lard or marmalade for lunch. And for dinner? Fried potatoes or a little cabbage. Maybe soup like this"—nodding toward the bowl in front of him. And then he added, with a sparkle in his eye: "But whatever you do, don't drink the cola. Demon urine!"

The young men flinched, looked at each other, eyed their bottled soft drinks in horror.

"*Es ist alles Scheisse*," added their good-humored neighbor, chuckling to himself. All shit.

Stephen looked around for a pay phone. His arrival time in L.A. was now uncertain. He must update Elaine. She would begin to worry. But there wasn't a phone anywhere. He would call her once he arrived at the airport, he decided.

Stephen excused himself to use the restroom. He walked to the back end of the place. The toilet was labelled *WC*. There was only one water closet for both men and women. He opened the door and went inside, lifted the seat, opened his fly and began to relieve himself. As he stood urinating, he read the graffiti on the walls: hieroglyphics scribbled, obscene sketches of men's and women's body parts. He closed his eyes. Involuntarily, images of Elaine flashed like glossy Hallmark cards: her soft belly, full breasts, the nape of her long neck, lustrous black hair …

He finished, zipped up, flushed the toilet, pushing down hard the rusty button on the top of the tank with an index finger. He turned on the faucet and washed his hands in cold water. There was no soap. Nor were there paper towels. He bent over and dried his hands on his pant legs, still damp from the rain. He opened the door.

When he returned to the dining area, the first thing he saw was the distinguished, good-humored stranger, standing and looking wide-eyed at Stephen, shaken.

Then Stephen scanned the room. The three students from Arizona State University were gone.

The old gentleman's eyes darted back and forth, looking first at the door, then at Stephen, then back at the door.

Stephen dashed to the door and pushed it open. He stepped outside the restaurant and gazed at the spot where the car had once been parked. Then he scanned the surroundings. The red Yugo, its three ephemeral passengers, his suitcase — gone.

Stephen watched as several birds, reacting in agitation to the sound of the restaurant's screen door slamming shut on its spring hinge, fluttered up deliriously toward the clearing sky, their beating wings and squawks creating a racket.

Then only silence.

– 55 –

Stephen sat up front in the Mercedes with the elderly gentleman, whose name he learned was Helmut Schmatloch. They rode for fifty minutes to Timișoara Airport.

All Stephen could think of as they traveled along the bumpy road was how he must have a guardian angel after all. What other explanation could there be for coming upon this good man, this savior of sorts, when he felt so utterly forsaken, potentially marooned in Moravița for God knows how long, down to his last two hundred dollars and a pocketful of nearly worthless Lions?

Schmatloch, a businessman whose home base was Frankfurt, told Stephen a shorthand version of why he was in Romania. "Like you, I had to jump ship when Belgrade Airport closed."

Stephen looked chagrined, recalling the tank, the soldiers.

"I know. It all seems so Paleozoic to us Westerners. But

you must understand. There was never an Enlightenment here."

"So then. Why Yugoslavia?" Stephen asked, puzzled. It was a country in upheaval.

"You mean why am I here? It's not the people of Yugoslavia or even the government that concerns us. Not their way of life, certainly. No, it's rather basic. It's their natural resources."

"Oil?"

"Not really. Yugoslav wells supply only twenty-six percent of domestic raw petroleum requirements. No—not oil. Not coal either. Yugoslavia, my friend, is rich in several nonferrous *metals*."

Stephen looked at him questioningly.

"Bauxite, lead, zinc, chrome, manganese, uranium, mercury ... The Yugoslavians may be poor, sadly, but the earth here is rich."

Stephen learned that Schmatloch was in Belgrade on behalf of a firm called Hoeschst, which was heavily involved in synthetic fibers and pharmaceuticals.

"In fact, most of Germany's commercial relations with Yugoslavia don't involve any government at all," the businessman said. "It's all company to company. But you see, people are worried about what happens tomorrow in the Balkan countries. If road traffic is cut off, for example—what then? Or, as you and I have just experienced, the airports are closed. Not very good for business. No indeed!"

"Okay," Stephen said. "I guess you guys are hightailing it out."

"We are. As far as new ventures go, there is no movement here. The risk is relatively high at this moment. Everybody is waiting for a political definition."

"Dinar and leu are pretty worthless. I've discovered that much."

"Quite so. Hyperinflation is the culprit. Yugoslavia has never been so close to a collapse of its economic system. Agriculture, industrial production—falling rapidly."

Stephen realized that he knew almost nothing about his host country or, for that matter, the world at large. He'd remained inside a cocoon made of celluloid under a canopy of false pretenses for much of his life.

Schmatloch asked Stephen many questions about his work in Yugoslavia, but Stephen left out the particulars, deliberately remaining vague, evasive. He did not quite know how to explain how he'd made so many wrong choices, how he'd broken his life apart into many jagged pieces, like a wine glass thrown to the floor.

"I'm sorry," said Stephen, addressing not only this man before him but also Elaine and Emily.

"No! It is understandable. These are harrowing times."

As they neared the airport, Schmatloch explained that he would drop off the car at the Kompas rental agency. He suggested that it would be best if he deposited Stephen at the Lufthansa terminal before returning the car; he could see that Stephen was anxious.

Stephen did not know what to say by way of thanks. This man's generosity left Stephen feeling indebted, immeasurably so, but there was nothing he could do.

"Hoeschst has a new subsidiary in the U.S., Hoeschst Celanese," said Schmatloch. "Who knows, eh, Stephen? We may meet again in your Los Angeles."

– 56 –

Stephen pushed through the main entrance doors and stepped into the terminal. A roar of echoes, induced by the relentless announcements on the P.A. system in myriad languages, and the chaotic sounds of a people in the throes of an exodus, flooded through him.

He asked a woman wearing a Lufthansa flight attendant's uniform if she knew where the pay phones were. She spoke English but with a heavy German accent that made a jumble of her explanation, sending him on a wild goose chase. He walked quickly to the end of the building, took a flight of stairs, came to a dead end in a passageway made of concrete and dark shadows. He looked frantically in every direction.

At last he located the phone booths arranged in a line like rigid wooden soldiers along one wall. He entered one and struggled with the phone, plunging silver King Carols and King Michaels rapidly into the slots, dialing the country code for the U.S.A. and his home number. At last the operator made the connection and he heard a pulsing ringing through the earpiece. The ringing continued for a full minute; no one picked up. Enormous pressure began mounting inside his head. There were any number of explanations for this. Elaine was at work, at the store, in the shower. He couldn't compute in his mind what time it was at home. He'd lost all sense of time.

He hung up the phone and ran back the way he'd come.

Although he waited in the Lufthansa check-in line for nearly two hours, he did not see Helmut Schmatloch anywhere. But then, perhaps Hoeschst provided him with a private jet, Stephen reasoned. That seemed likely. That would make sense. The regal businessman was a man of influence, a man of importance. Stephen admired the man; he was everything Stephen wasn't. He had money—the Mercedes, the designer clothing. He had dignity, self-respect. He clearly knew what he was doing.

Nor did Stephen spot the young thieves from Arizona State. He wasn't sure what he'd do if he came across them.

Stephen tried to send his thoughts elsewhere but could not. First, he tried to conjure up the image of lilacs. That effort failed. He thought about the last scene of the movie, the naked actors, Trueblood like Emperor Nero playing fiddle as Stephen's movie burned—terrifying ideas kept intruding on his thoughts. He tried not to think about what would happen when he reached the ticket counter: what if the credit card had already reached its limit? What *was* the limit? He had no idea. What would happen if the card was rejected? What then? What would he do? How would he get home on two hundred dollars?

But his luck held. The ticket purchase cleared. Once home, he would thank Elaine for her good money management skills, her great work ethic, her profound wisdom in all things.

He stepped away from the desk and looked down at his itinerary, studied it …

Timișoara, Romania (TSR-Traian Vuia)

Sun, March 12, 1989
From
Traian Vuia (TSR)
To
Los Angeles Intl. (LAX)

Lufthansa
6:20 p.m.
TSR
To
3:05 pm
LAX
30 h 45m, 1 stop
MUC
Arrives Mon March 13, 1989

Trip Total: $1,570.33

They would fly to Franz Josef Strauss International Airport in Munich, a 90-minute flight. Okay, thought Stephen. This is a small airport. No direct flights. So be it.

Then Stephen looked more closely. The layover in Munich was seventeen hours and fifteen minutes. There would be no hotel, not when his funds were so precariously low. He would have to camp out in the terminal.

Seventeen lost hours, then the 12-hour flight to L.A.—the last measure of the gauntlet. He would have plenty of time to plot revenge.

– 57 –

Stephen had a window seat. A German-speaking couple sat next to him. The woman was obese and straddled the middle seat, her arm and thigh spilling over into Stephen's space, forcing him to lean hard to the right, awkwardly, on the armrest. He remained in this position, lopsided, for the duration of the flight.

Once they reached cruising altitude, the plane leveled off. Rain streaked across the small window. Stephen gazed out at the gray void. Lightning began filling the sky with flashes, blinding, apocalyptic. The plane suddenly bucked violently. The seatbelt sign ahead lit up brightly, an urgent flashing, feverish red.

A male flight attendant's voice announced, first in German, then in English: "*Bitte schnallen Sie sich an. Das Flugzeug ist auf einige Turbulenzen gestossen* ... Please fasten your seat belts. The plane has encountered some turbulence."

Stephen closed his eyes, but it was too late. The lightning, bright zigzagging explosions in the firmament outside the plane, triggered electrical discharges in his brain. The outside world became the within. Consequently, he experienced a full-blown migraine. Severe pain throbbed in the left hemisphere of his skull. Sounds around him became like nails driven into his inner ears. Nausea soon followed. He lay back against the seat, twisting away from his neighbor in the middle seat, paralyzed by pain. The pain in his head was excruciating. He clenched his eyelids closed. But he kept seeing blinding light.

And yet, despite his infirmity, there was something vaguely mystical about physical suffering—something powerful and indomitable. He wondered: Had Saint Paul experienced something like this when he was struck blind and thrown off his horse on the road to Damascus?

But no voice from heaven came.

Helpless in this condition, Stephen could not stop the deluge of images that appeared in his mind. He suddenly saw his wife and daughter. He could picture their faces, but they were severe glares—dead eyes, staring like dead fish—without smiles. Then they dissolved into police mug shots. Much as he tried to will the images away, he could not erase their reprimanding looks.

So he became philosophical. Everything happened the way it had happened. There would be no changing, let alone erasing, the past. He could not turn back the clock. These were immutable, terrifying forces at work—like hurricanes or tornadoes, stemming from within and from without, larger than himself—that had been subsumed into his life. Once he told Elaine what happened to the money and how he'd left the movie unfinished, she would see him for what he was: a fraud. He'd spent more money on this venture than he'd made; he'd endangered his family by working for hoodlums; he'd betrayed her—these were irrefutable facts. There was nothing he could do to erase them.

He must accept the consequences, and he knew they would be severe.

– PART FOUR –
WRAP PARTY

– 58 –

After killing seventeen hours in Munich Airport—dozing on a bench at the departure gate, eating an Egg McMuffin and an order of World Famous Fries, drinking two "grande" cups of Starbucks coffee in hopes of bringing relief to his aching head—Stephen finally flew home.

During the flight, Stephen had no thoughts at all; he stared blankly at the closed overhanging luggage compartment door closest to him for most of the trip. Then he remembered his suitcase: now somewhere in a Romanian dumpster, no doubt, and its contents—thousands of dollars and a few articles of clothing—scavenged.

It was Colon's fault. Everything. He was behind everything. The betrayals, the losses, the suffering.

There would be retribution.

Just before landing, he made a final trip to the restroom at the rear of the plane. Inside the tiny compartment, he strove to repair his disheveled appearance, running a comb he'd bought at the Munich airport through his hair. He'd also purchased a toothbrush and a small tube of toothpaste; he brushed his teeth. He wiped his armpits with soap from the dispenser and wet paper towels, then dried them and applied deodorant.

He wasn't going to face his wife, after having not seen her for over a month and after all he'd been through, without at least looking somewhat decent.

− 59 −

Stephen found a pay phone at LAX. He forced quarters into the slot and punched in his home phone number. It rang four times, then:

"*Hello*" — Elaine's electronic voice. To his surprise, she'd bought an answering machine. What else had she done while he was gone? he wondered. Would the apartment look different somehow? New curtains? Furniture? No, there was no money for that. The answering machine may have been the FBI's idea. "*I can't come to the phone right now ...*"

When Stephen heard the beep tone at last, he shouted into the mouthpiece: "Elaine! It's Stephen. I'm at the airport. It's Monday, I don't know, about four o'clock. I'm here! I'll be right home. I'll catch a cab ..." It wasn't a shout; it was a roar. Heads in the terminal turned.

He hung up the phone, got through the press of harried throng, followed the signs indicating the way to the exit. He would not need to visit baggage claim.

He was still wearing the clothes he'd donned on Saturday morning. He smelled like the stale cigarettes at the

Munich airport. He scanned the area for a shop selling clothing and found one. *America 1* sold gift items, including an Air Force One toy plane and Commander in Chief accessories. They also carried a T-shirt with *U.S.A.* printed across the front. He paid cash for it, then changed in the men's room, tossing his old shirt into the waste bin. At least he'd *smell* okay and look *presentable.*

A line of taxis awaited him outside the terminal. As he walked quickly toward a yellow cab at the head of the line, the driver, a man who looked to be in his late forties and was possibly a Middle Eastern immigrant—he was wearing a Peshawari turban—stepped out of the cab, circled around it, and opened the passenger door for Stephen. He climbed in.

As they drove off, Stephen asked the man where he was from. The man replied, "Pakistan."

The drive up Century Boulevard took them past an In-N-Out burger stand; several hotels and car parking structures; a billboard advertising the Spearmint Rhino Gentlemen's Club, with the colossal face of a heavily mascaraed and crimson-lipsticked woman looking demure and available; a McDonald's; a Union 76 gas station; a Denny's; car rental companies: Avis, Thrifty, Enterprise—all a blur as Stephen looked straight ahead, not focusing on anything in particular, just a random point in space.

"The fastest way is the Ten freeway, I believe," said the driver, gazing over the back of his seat. (This was long before GPS navigation. The drivers then would have to rely on their expert knowledge of the city, and on their instincts.) "But it is no longer in mileage—not as the bird flies. The more direct way is Lincoln Boulevard, but it is slow this time, especially as it is rush hour. But then again, the freeway may be a parking lot. It is always a gamble. This is L.A." He said the city's name as if it were one exotic word: "Elay."

"The freeway," said Stephen without hesitation. Lincoln Boulevard was always a crawl, and the thousand-and-one stop lights ...

He would be home in an hour, he calculated. Each silent mile on the way home would give him more might, more potency. The stronger he appeared to Elaine, he imagined, the better. It would only bolster her respect for him. His main weapon of self-defense would be his unwavering, rock-solid convictions: he must rescue his little family, must unleash his fury on the man who'd brought all this down on him. But he must first assure Elaine of his undying love for her.

He began rehearsing in his mind what he'd say to her when they finally reunited.

– 60 –

The driver pulled up in front of the Riva Apartments on Sixth Street. Stephen thanked the driver, paid him, and exited the car.

He stood outside the stucco building. It was an ugly thing. Its architecture was a failed attempt at sixties modern and the outside walls always reminded Stephen of an iguana's leathery skin.

But it was home.

There were only a few parking spaces underneath a wooden pergola structure. Elaine's white Ford Windstar minivan, trimmed with a thin red band circumventing its body so that it resembled a Red Cross emergency vehicle, was nowhere in sight. If she wasn't home, he'd have a problem: he was without a key to the apartment.

He walked up the short flight of stairs and stepped up to the door. It had been a long journey. He was tired. But he was here: home. He held his breath for a moment, then released it.

He would try the doorknob, and if it was locked, he would knock softly. If no one was there, he would sit on the doorstep and wait.

But the door opened easily when he turned the knob and pushed. He was surprised, even a little irritated. Elaine was usually cautious. Santa Monica was a big city; it had its share of crime. *Something is wrong.*

As he took a step into his apartment, the first thing his senses registered was the smell: rosemary, basil, garlic was it?—and *my God*, was that lilac? Had Elaine bought flowers and placed them in a vase? Then he heard a faint sound: someone humming the tune to Janet Jackson's song "Miss You Much."

The kitchen was positioned on the other side of a wall—a short hallway.

"Elaine!" he called out. The humming stopped. He walked down the hallway. He turned the corner and faced the kitchen.

A woman was standing at the stove, her back to him, stirring something in a large stockpot with a wooden ladle. Hair color different: blonde. Something was all wrong. She stopped stirring.

Now Elaine turned and faced Stephen.

Except it wasn't Elaine.

"Stephen," she said joyfully. "You're home! Thank Hecate you're safe!"

"Diane," said Stephen, barely audible—he was dumb-founded. He blinked as if dazed, disoriented—in a state of shock. *What the hell?*

"What are you doing here?" he said at last. He looked around the apartment, as if he'd stepped into the wrong one somehow. He recognized the furniture. This certainly was his home—*their* home. "Where's Elaine?"

Diane was wearing the same white pajamas she'd worn the last time he visited her in her Venice apartment on the way to the airport. Stephen stood there, jaw slack, mouth open.

"I got your message," she said, "On the answering machine. I was so excited—"

"Where is she?" he snapped back at her. His face was flushed. His befuddlement was replaced by outrage.

"Who, Stephen? Who are you looking for?"—stated in mock innocence.

"You know who," he replied finally. Her question had filled him with horror. He glared at her. His eyes were wild. "Diane," he said, voice dropping into a near whisper as he struggled to contain his fury. "Where's Elaine? Where's Emily?"

She shook her head and smiled. It was a smile like a knife. The whites of her eyes were luminous in the florescent kitchen light. "They're gone," she said, eerily cheerful. "So we're free now, Stephen. That woman won't bother us anymore." *That woman.*

"Nonono …" he said, his throat tightening with panic.

"Just think. You're a free man in, maybe not Paris, but in L.A. now." Then she started to sing cheerfully about not needing a piece of paper from the city hall.

"Stop it!" he thundered.

She looked surprised. "It's your favorite, isn't it? Joni Mitchell? At least one of your favorites?"

Feelings of hatred and rage were gradually metamorphosing into a new emotion. He looked at Diane with outright disgust now. He was consumed by repulsion. He closed his eyes and thought about his history with her, all in a moment. She'd been so good at staying out of his world, never prying, she'd been so good, never calling the house ...

Then, suddenly, he understood.

"Wait a minute. Diane ... it was you, wasn't it?" Repulsion now blossomed into epiphany.

"What? It was me *what*?"

"You were the one calling the house. *You* were the one threatening to kidnap Emily ..."

She smiled, pleased with herself. "Well, you have to admit, Stephen. It worked. I mean, *look*! You're *here*! She's *gone*!"

"Wait a second ..." He thought about it. She was mad. Could he believe anything this woman said? "Elaine said it was a man who kept calling."

She laughed, shook her head dismissively. "A friend of mine, a fellow Wiccan—a *warlock*, to be exact. Warlocks use black magic against others."

She was happy. She seemed proud of herself. She'd

accomplished everything she'd desired: she'd replaced the wife.

"I thought you might like this hairstyle," she said, placing a hand on the top of her hair. Something was different about it, he decided. The bangs were new. Severe bowl-cut bangs. "It's the Joni Mitchell look. I thought you'd like it. Incredibly sexy, you think?" She struck a pose, tilting her head to the side, hand still on her head, smiling. She searched his face for a verdict.

He suddenly looked tired. The weariness of a long, drawn-out illness.

"What happened, Diane? Just tell me."

Maintaining her model's pose, she curled her hair behind her left ear with two fingers, revealing an earring with an emerald stone. Stephen stared at it—first perplexed, then suddenly horrified.

"Recognize them?" she asked.

He did.

"Elaine gave them to me," explained Diane. "She said they were a gift from you on your first anniversary."

"*What the hell!!*" he screamed.

The journey he'd made to find … this. His life turned on its head. Life wasn't supposed to unfold this way. If you had loved many women, the only one facing you at this juncture in your life, right here, right now, should be the one you loved the most. Your true love. Not this woman occupying his kitchen. An actress playing the starring role—of wife.

"Elaine was very *very* angry with you."

Blood rose to his face. He closed his eyes and let his chin drop to his chest. He wasn't feeling well at all. The hot flush of fever was growing from within.

She crossed over to him and placed her hands on his shoulders. She wrinkled her nose and frowned as she looked him over.

"You're a mess. I'm going to get you in a nice hot bath. Maybe toss in some nice aromatic mineral salts. Make you a new man. Make you a *man*."

"Diane, please—" He look defeated, body sagging. Shamefacedness.

"But first I want you to try this amazing dish. Tagliatelle con ragu Bolognese." She walked back to the stove, retrieved the ladle, and began stirring the mixture. "It's a spaghetti sauce I made myself! Aren't you proud of me?"

He just stared.

"People will tell you to make sauces in metal pots. Some say it *disrupts the energy of the herbs*. I have to say, I totally disagree. I've had a lot of success with these cast iron pots."

"Please …"

She went on: "It seems to me that the iron practically *vibrates* with the energies within, and lends the grounding of the Element of Earth."

"Diane!!" he screamed at her.

"Okay," she sighed, caving in—perhaps out of sympathy; he was clearly suffering. She brought the ladle to her lips and tasted the sauce. She nodded approvingly, put down the ladle. Then she turned back to Stephen, crossing her arms in front of her chest.

"It was simple. I just came over to your—*our* apartment, it's *our* apartment now, I can afford the rent, we'll just change the rental agreement—and I sat down with Elaine over a cup of tea. She's really a very fine woman, Stephen—but clearly not your type. She's very …" She thought deeply, closing her eyes, then opened them and met his gaze, as if challenging him to disagree. "She's very regal. Regal? Is that the right word? Very formal … *queenly*," she said, at last satisfied with the word choice. "I liked her."

He fought for breath. Everything good in his life he'd worked for, *suffered* for, wiped away.

"You told her," he said, the words sighed rather than spoken. "About us."

"I thought she should know. We sisters have to stick together. She does not deserve to be deceived. No woman deserves betrayal by her man. She's a good woman—just not the *right* woman for you. I think you need a wife not so, hmmm … lofty? Intellectual? Aloof? Ethereal? I don't know. *You're* the writer—a *screenwriter*, aren't you, Stephen? Is that the right word, ethereal?" She searched through her mind. Then: "No. I've got it. *Angelic*! That's it." She smiled knowingly, raising an eyebrow. "Forget angels. I think you like your women more …"—a cunning look now—"down to earth. Isn't that right, Stephen?"

"You—are—crazy," he said, voice flat.

"Poor Stephen," she sighed, walking toward him, a hint of sadness glinting in her watering eyes. "What am I going to do with you?" She reached out to him as if to comfort him, as if he were a little boy.

"Don't touch me," he snarled, recoiling from her.

He suddenly turned and dashed into their bedroom, his and Elaine's. He quickly crossed over to the small writing desk set against a wall. The first thing that caught his eye on his way there was a photo in a picture frame, center stage on the dresser. It was a snapshot of himself, wearing a black suit and black tie; Elaine in a cobalt-blue satin dress; and two-year-old Emily in a green velvet dress and white tights. Stephen remembered the setting well. They were standing outside the little church, the Noe Valley Ministry. You could see it in the background behind them: simple, small, gray façade, elegant steeple. They'd just been married. Stephen remembered the Celebrant saying to Emily during the ceremony:

"Today, in a very special way, a family is affirmed and publicly united. Emily is a special part of this bonding of this family relationship. Emily, do you accept this family to be yours?" Emily had hugged Stephen and Elaine, Stephen recalled. And he'd written the vows himself:

> *I, Stephen, take you, Elaine, to be my wedded wife. I promise to love you, in faith and in trust, to respect you, care for you, and stand by your side, through sorrow and joy, through struggle and prosperity, for all the days of our lives.*

He actually remembered all this. It had come back to him in a rush. He also remembered that they'd ended the

ceremony with a reading of a poem. It was an Apache Wedding Blessing — Elaine's idea. Stephen recalled a fragment:

> *Now you will feel no rain,*
> *For each of you*
> *Will be shelter to the other.*

He leaned in, looked closer at the 8x10 photograph.
Emily's tights were torn at the left knee, a small tear; she'd
tripped and fallen to the ground as they were leaving the
church. There was a little blood discernible on the white
material just below the knee; her cheeks were wet with
tears. He remembered the day in an instant.

He turned back to the desk. Elaine would do her account-
ing here. This corner of the apartment was her domain. He
opened both drawers one after the other, rapidly rummaging
through the stacks of paper, the bills, envelopes, checkbook,
yellow stickies, erasers, paper clips, pens …

He found what he was looking for: Elaine's address
book. He picked it up, opened it, began turning the pages,
searching … his eyes soon settled on a notation, written in
Elaine's wonderfully intricate, elegant cursive handwriting:

Ted Hathwater
7222 Avenida de la Entrada, Ojai

Stephen tore the page out of the little book and folded
it in half, tucked it into his pocket.

This will take discipline and focus, he decided. He concentrated …

Diane was standing at the door, blocking his exit. He rushed to the door and pushed her aside with a sweep of his arm as he ran out of the bedroom. "Stephen!" she cried out after him as he returned to the kitchen, eyes quickly scanning, and then he saw her purse resting on the counter by the sink. He opened it and frenetically began digging through it until he found her car keys. He held them up and looked carefully at the round medallion dangling from the keychain. It read *Honda.*

"What are you doing?" Diane asked, standing close behind him now, hands on hips, watching—a witch's wrath in her eye.

"Ellie!" he bellowed to the ceiling, to the rooftops, to his wife miles away.

He ran down the hall and out the door. He bounded down the steps and landed hard on the asphalt of the carport, causing him to grunt. He looked about, searching for a Honda. A white Civic was parked across the street. He ran to it and tried the key in the door's keyhole. It fit nicely. He twisted the key, and the lock clicked audibly. He opened the door and climbed in behind the wheel. The interior smelled of Diane.

He inserted the key into the ignition and started up the car. He looked at the fuel gauge. Half full. Enough to get him to Ojai.

– 61 –

He hardly noticed the ocean, illuminated as it was by a full moon, looking iridescent, after the 101 became Highway 1 at Ventura. His mind was consumed with concocting various scenarios. What would he say and do when he confronted Elaine? What words could ever repair the damage he'd inflicted on his family? What tone of voice should he adopt when speaking to her? Humility seemed the appropriate stance. Apologies would not suffice; he would have to beg for her forgiveness, cry crocodile tears. It would have to be an Oscar-caliber performance. He thought of Marlon Brando in *Last Tango in Paris*, weeping and cursing over his wife lying in state.

The houses of Ojai village nestle in the valley like eggs in a bird's nest. The town is situated in a small, east-west valley about 15 miles from Ventura and the Pacific coast. Its name means *nest* in the Chumash Indian language. California's own Shangri-La. An endless expanse of turquoise sky above palm-lined streets, whitewashed and red-tiled Spanish Revival architecture, yoga studios, acres of citrus and avocado orchards—if not Shangri-La, then perhaps Eden.

It took Stephen an hour and a half to get there from Santa Monica. It was early evening. The sun was down, the sky still aglow—"magic hour," as cinematographers call it. The stars were just beginning to appear, in abundance.

Stephen pulled the Honda over to the side of the road and stopped. A new Ferrari and a battered biodiesel Mercedes with a hubcap missing were parked nearby. A world of extremes: the have and have-nots, the rich and the homeless: the schizophrenic nature of the place.

But beautiful. If only he were in the right state of mind to appreciate it. Stephen saw nothing more than a blankness, strange surroundings that posed a challenge: how to find Uncle Ted's place. That's all. He had an address, but he would need directions in this maze of small-town streets, dirt roads, orchards.

He remembered: most people carried maps, Thomas Guides, in their cars. Stephen turned in his seat and bent down to inspect the floor behind him. Sure enough: Diane had one tucked halfway under the driver's seat. He brought it up and placed the spiral-bound atlas stuffed with street maps on his lap. He turned on the overhead light. The cover read *The Thomas Guide 1989 Los Angeles County Street Guide and Directory,* and this was Ventura County. The guide was useless.

A young man with yellow sun-bleached hair, wearing Ray-Ban sunglasses even at nightfall, lemon-colored shorts, flip-flops on his feet, and a T-shirt with the words *Chick Magnet* emblazoned across his chest, walked by the car. Stephen rolled down the window and leaned his head out.

"Excuse me," he said.

The young man stopped, turned, and looked back at Stephen, tilting his head down and peering over the sunglasses.

"Can you tell me where I can find—" Stephen pulled out the torn piece of paper from his pocket, checked it, looked back at the stranger—"Avenida de la Entrada?"

The young man pointed up the street, then described a complicated series of rights and lefts, which Stephen did his best to allocate to memory.

"Thanks," said Stephen. The stranger gave him a fleeting look of apprehension; there was clearly something amiss, something wrong with this person sitting behind the wheel. Was it the crazed look?

Stephen put the car into gear.

– 62 –

Stephen pulled up to the house and stopped the car on the gravel driveway. He peered through the windshield. He was startled by the expanse of the place; Elaine had described it, but he'd never seen it. She'd been ambiguous in her description, though, downplaying its opulence. Elaine and her brother were not close; his alcoholism and unpredictable mood swings, his violent tendencies, had pretty much rendered him *persona non grata*; she had a young daughter to protect, after all.

He got out of the car and looked around. It was a renovated 1920s Spanish Hacienda-style one-story spread hidden among acres of avocado trees, with stone walls, gardens, swimming pool, guest house, terrace. The six-thousand-foot Topatopa Mountains, the rim of the nest, were bathed in moonlight, forming an enchanting backdrop. And parked in an open carport was his wife's Windstar.

He walked around the Honda and made his way to the front door. He pressed the doorbell button and heard a chime from within. He waited.

A full minute later, the door opened. A tall man—well over six feet, in his fifties, a gray three-day beard and head as bald as a melon—opened it. Muscular build, his face dark and peppered with eraserhead-sized brown spots from years of exposure to the sun. Elaine had told Stephen that Ted had made a small fortune in real estate; he'd clearly worked a lot outdoors. Perhaps he spent his leisure time sunbathing on the terrace, downing margaritas all day. He was wearing a tank top that exposed his tanned broad shoulders: a surfer's build, Stephen speculated. Brutish, looking to Stephen more like a club bouncer than a surfer.

The man blocked the doorway, an impregnable human barrier, and looked Stephen up and down warily.

"Uncle Ted," said Stephen.

The man nodded knowingly. "Something tells me you are Stephen."

Stephen said nothing.

"Elaine's talked plenty about you, but I thought maybe she made it all up. But you're real. So, hey. How come you never come visit?"

"I could say the same about you."

"Yeah. I guess you're right." Ted smiled. "I guess you and I aren't too social."

Stephen wanted to say it was because Ted was a mean drunk and Elaine wanted to spare Stephen any trouble. She meant to protect Stephen and her child.

Instead of inviting him in, the big man quickly stepped out of the doorway and placed a weighty arm around Stephen's shoulders, gently but forcefully turning him away from the house. For Stephen, a much smaller man, there was no resisting.

Uncle Ted spoke as he aggressively led Stephen out onto the driveway:

"Have you been to Ojai before, Stephen, or is this it?" — jovially, as if all were right with the world. It was the sort of tactic often used by police when attempting to diffuse a tense situation.

Stephen said nothing. He glanced over his shoulder at the house as Ted guided him toward the car.

"Lately a new wave of, shall we say, transplants?—I say this euphemistically—city dwellers, riffraff is more precise—they've moved in," Ted said in an instructor's—or therapist's—modulated tone of voice. "Farm-to-table biker bars. Small inns. Pop-up crafts fairs. It's become a kind of hippie utopia. It's all turned to shit." He shook his head and clicked his tongue in disgust.

They stopped alongside the Honda. He lifted his heavy arm from Stephen's shoulders, releasing him, and turned to face him. "If you're wondering how I acquired all this, it took some work. I got into real estate. Sis tell you that? I bet you never knew that. Elaine probably told you I stole it or something. Robbed a bank. Anyway, I've been working with properties for the past thirty years—"

Stephen bolted toward the house.

He reached the front door, still open, and entered the house.

Uncle Ted entered behind him and stopped abruptly.

It was too late.

Stephen stood still, facing her. The two of them were still as department store mannequins.

Elaine Elizabeth Krawczyk (née Dorsey) stood barefoot on the Spanish tiles in the middle of the parlor. She was dressed in baggy gray sweatpants and a plain white T-shirt—a size extra-large, a man's shirt. Her dark hair was pulled back in a ponytail, and she was wearing no makeup. No smile, no expression of emotion, barely a look of recognition. He knew that look instantly: the passport photo in his migraine-tortured vision on the flight home.

"Please. Let me explain, Elaine—"

"Don't bother." A tear slid slowly down her face.

"I am so sorry," he began, searching for words, improvising, hoping for inspiration, waiting for the muses to speak. He'd rehearsed several speeches on the flight, but all of them were lost under a flood of emotion.

"I don't do well with cheating," she said undemonstratively, as if she were commenting on furniture fabric: I'm not much of a stripes person. She had a worn, exhausted look.

"I don't love that woman—"

"I'm done, Stephen."

"—she's horrible! Out of her mind. It was stupid, stupid, *stupid*—"

"Please go."

"You're the only woman I've ever loved, Ellie. I fell in love with *you*—just you, nobody else. You are the woman of my dreams"—pleading now.

She just smiled, face tear stained, and shook her head. Nothing more to be said.

Stephen was about to take a step toward her when he heard a door open nearby. A man entered the parlor. He was tall, with the body of a football player: a lean, sturdy quarterback. He had blond hair draping across his shoulders and halfway down his back, a beard—a jaunty Jesus.

Stephen immediately knew who this man was, although he'd only spoken a dozen words to him in the past two years. Elaine and her ex-husband stood side by side, in a clear demonstration of—what? Some kind of unity of purpose?

No one spoke. They stared coldly at Stephen. Dead-fish stare.

And then Emily, now four years old—it'd been two years since the wedding; he'd been her dad for two years—joined her biological mother and father, completing the tableau. She placed herself between them and took hold of each parent's hand. The image of them standing before him, forming a solid, harmonious composition, shocked Stephen. It was an image he would never forget: stock still and expressionless, like a daguerreotype from the nineteenth century. Fixed and irreversible.

The image became seared into his brain, a branding, an invisible X that would mark him for the rest of his life.

— 63 —

Stephen drove to the coast in a trance. He had no idea how he managed to get there.

He parked the car and got out. The sign said VENTURA HARBOR VILLAGE MARINA. He'd been there only once before, a day trip up the coast, a "fun outing" with Elaine and Emily, long ago. He remembered Elaine calling the nearby Channel Islands the "American Galapagos." You could see the islands from the shoreline. He did not know what she meant and failed to extract an explanation. But he was impressed. She struck him as a smart, clever woman.

He took in his surroundings. The Ventura Harbor complex included administration facilities, the marina center, a resort hotel, parking areas, boat ramps, a sport fishing center, a boat repair yard, restaurants, marina hardware, and a mobile home park. Approximately 1,500 craft, most of them sport fishing boats and commercial fishing vessels, were moored in the harbor. On this spot he could only take in a fraction of its offerings.

Stephen walked into the marina and found the docks.

He took a seat on a bench within view of a splendid yacht.

He spent the night on this spot, only leaving it once to use a public restroom nearby. He sat near the water watching the sailboats in the moonlight, gently rocking in their berths. It was long after closing time, but no one asked him to leave. It was as if he were invisible.

Sometime well after midnight he spotted a tennis ball lodged at the base of a gate that blocked a ramp leading down to a sailboat. He got up and crossed over to it, bent down and picked up the ball. Were there tennis courts here too?

He returned to the bench, holding the ball in his right hand. He sat there squeezing it. He recalled that his dad would use a V-shaped hand device with a resistance spring as part of his daily exercise regimen. It was supposed to strengthen muscles, reduce stress, lower blood pressure, even prevent dementia, his dad had explained. Squeeze hard and hold for ten seconds, his dad had said. Slowly release for ten seconds. Repeat. Stephen squeezed and released the ball ten times, then threw it down the length of the causeway, where it bounced and eventually rolled into the water.

The ocean breeze drove cold dampness clean through his thin jacket, his *U.S.A.* T-shirt from the airport, his jeans, and into the cells of his body. He shivered. He was also very tired, his body sagging with fatigue. He thought he might be getting a fever. He slowly lay down on the bench. He remained still for what felt like a very long time.

• • •

He did not recall falling asleep, but he must have, despite the biting cold, the tightness in the gut, the painful branding of the mark.

He had to be dreaming.

He was standing in the lobby of the Hotel Jugoslavija in Belgrade. The great chandelier hung overhead, its five thousand lightbulbs blazing, all forty thousand crystals sparkling, 24-carat diamonds in the light.

The crew and cast of *Infernal Beauty* gathered in the lobby for the production wrap party. Others were still streaming in through the massive front doors. There were about 120 people dressed to the nines. He recognized them all. Lorenzo shook his hand vigorously. *"Congratulazion!"* he said. "Jennifer" kissed him sweetly on the cheek and thanked him for his brilliant directorial guidance. Max Trueblood kissed him on both cheeks, in the Roman way.

They made their way into the grand ballroom and took their places at enormous round tables. Stephen, the guest of honor, sat at a table with all the producers, Yugoslavian and Italian, Borko and Colon included, all of whom were filled with mirth and good cheer. Colon smiled broadly, revealing those jagged teeth, the color of egg yolks. A feast had been flown in all the way from Rome—battered zucchini flowers stuffed with mozzarella and anchovies; Bacalla from Dar Filettaro, salted cod fried in an eggy batter, artichokes braised and stuffed with herbs and sprinkled with lemon; carbonara from Rome's legendary Roscioli restaurant, with its creamy egg-based sauce dotted with pieces of succulent cured pork jowl; dumplings of all varieties from Estonia

and Lithuania; and the best champagnes in the world: Krug
Clos du Mesnil de Blanc Brut ...

At one point in the evening, after the enchanted array
of desserts had been served and consumed, Trueblood
called for a screening of outtakes and bloopers, a tradition
at wrap parties. Stephen watched as a five-by-five-foot
screen was erected in the dining room and a projector
placed on a table. Then he watched images flicker on the
sparkly white surface: actors flubbing their lines, the boom
operator accidentally stepping into a shot, a set piece falling
over, Stephen appearing in a take, yelling at someone and
waving his arms in exasperation. In this shot he turns to
the camera. He draws his right hand across his throat, the
gesture signaling self-decapitation, and shouts "Cut!"

He awoke with a violent shudder. Stephen opened his eyes.
Where was he?

He felt soul-sickness. His stomach ached with hunger
too; he hadn't eaten anything since the Lufthansa flight.
He looked around, sat up, blinked several times. It took
some time for him to orient himself. Then he remembered
everything.

Home? Not Santa Monica. Not anymore.

Anyone passing by would have taken him for a homeless person. He looked the part: disheveled, godforsaken.
With the earth cut away from under his feet, he found
himself alone and adrift.

He looked up at the night sky. Sick with fear and loss,

he withered under the moon's bright glower.

Then he remembered: he still had Elaine's credit card. It was all he had of value in the world. He retrieved his wallet from a jacket pocket and found the card, plucked it out and held it before him with both hands, as if it were a host and he were a priest performing Holy Communion. But it belonged to Elaine, it was her card and the only one that hadn't been canceled by the banks. It belonged to her. So he folded it in half, folded it back and forth several times, then tore it down the middle. He tossed the two halves in a trashcan nearby.

Then the car key. He dug the key chain out of his pants pocket. Diane's Honda—he was a car thief now. Attached to the chain was a tiny medallion. He examined it closely. The medallion had the image of a five-pointed star within a circle imprinted on it—a Wiccan symbol. He threw the key chain as hard as he could in the same direction as the tennis ball. He could hear the faint sound of the keys kerplunking into the water.

He sat back down on the bench. He rubbed away the discharge caked in the corners of his eyes and tried to focus. Tried to think …

Then he saw her. A young woman, in her early twenties, he guessed, walked up the dock toward him. She did not see him, though; she was looking out at the boats, and he was invisible. She walked with her back so straight and her head held so high that he imagined she must be a ballerina. The effortless, graceful way she carried herself caused him to hold his breath.

She stopped at a gate at the top of a boat ramp. She reached inside her pants pocket and pulled out a key, which she engaged in a large padlock. It snapped open. Unwrapping a heavy chain, she pulled the gate toward her.

He watched her as she made her way down the steep grade of the ramp. At the bottom, using a stepladder, she climbed aboard the boat—a magnificent sailing vessel, a 42-foot Hunter 420 Passage. He imagined it must be worth well over six figures. Seven? He watched her partake in what must be a boat owner's typical daily ritual: maintenance.

He kept watching. What to do? He couldn't go home. There was no going back. No removing the branded X …

He breathed in the briny sea air, letting his lungs expand fully, then breathed out. The sun had just risen. It was a beautiful day. He smiled.

He would start over again. A phoenix rising from the ashes.

He stood up and began walking. He came to the unlocked gate and pulled it open. He then made his way down the ramp, slowly, quietly, careful not to startle her, never taking his eyes off the woman as she began the long and arduous job of oiling the boat's sun-bleached teak deck, her long golden hair capturing the sun and radiating light.

Acknowledgments

I owe a great debt to the talented, dedicated and energetic souls at Meadowlark Publishing Services, and especially to Stanton Nelson, who read the manuscript and suggested all manner of corrections and adjustments, some quite subtle but all immeasurably beneficial to the cause; his unerring good judgment went far beyond the mere page. As always, I owe incalculable thanks to my wife, Marcy, the brightest star in the firmament, for believing in me during the movie-making years, even when I lost faith, and even more so for supporting my more recent writing endeavors, unfailingly standing by me with grace; and to Olivia, for offering moral support and wise advice during good times and bad, especially amid a pandemic. Drew Maddock too stepped forward—it was his rich experience gained while traveling in the Balkans during the eighties that provided much welcomed detail to the story—as did Heath Moon, who offered frank advice tempered by his trademark kindness.

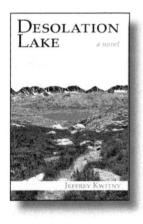

CPSIA information can be obtained
at www.ICGtesting.com
Printed in the USA
BVHW062213010321
601388BV00005B/541

9 781736 416600